Harvest Protocol

Spectral Hunter Series

Morgan Kessler

A Little Vast Studios, LLC

Contents

Prologue

On the condo rental app, the host listed "country silence and privacy" as a selling point, though Alexei doubted that most guests appreciated silence the way he did. Moscow Mills, Missouri, is one of those rural satellites a half-hour drive from any meaningful city. The scenery here isn't all that amazing, just flat and wide and sometimes erased entirely by morning fog. The main street is laughable—seven businesses in a row, then fields—but the rental home is, as advertised, "nicely furnished."

There is an irony in this place he finds pleasurable. Moscow Mills, named by some ambitious 19th-century miller who wanted his flour to seem foreign and superior. The town was never Russian, not even a little. Alexei learned this from the town library's lone staff member, a woman in a cardigan decorated with cats. She told him the story in one uninterrupted paragraph, then repeated it verbatim, as if delivering a Wikipedia entry twice guaranteed its truth.

Procedure completed, Alexei takes off his gloves long enough to confirm the Deliverer's work is done, via his phone. He could tell his buyer was not on the other end of their texts. Not directly, at least. Their little coded messages came through an intermediary, who wrote in clipped but at least Russian Cyrillic. Guess they wanted to eliminate and chance of miscommunication. The message was, as with the previous lists, simple: eight possible subjects from the list of one hundred. Of those, tonight's man was number one.

What was his name again? Barry? Larry? Something like that.

The guy wasn't even fifty kilos; he thinks. He recalls his app profile claimed 135 pounds, which is close enough, but in person the man's wrists look like chopsticks and his forearms show the filaments of blue vein just beneath the skin. Alexei reads these cues instinctively—years of clinical training imprinted the taxonomy of human bodies onto his brain, so that he now classifies strangers first by bone density, blood flow, subdermal fat.

Alexei takes a moment to affix new gloves and admire his harvest: the pink, healthy liver, the kidneys so smooth and flawless it seems obscene to have removed them.

But therein lies their value.

He weighs the liver by feel. Alexei knows from the chart it should be 1,450 grams; his hands tell him he is correct within a hundred. He rinses it in chilled saline, then slides it into the first of the prepared coolers, the preservation solution biting his knuckles with its cold.

Seventy-five thousand US dollars for this, he thinks, and suppresses a smile. Back home, he couldn't have earned that in three years.

He moves on to the kidneys—both excellent, both unscarred. They will probably fetch considerably less, since they're not on his patron's shopping list. But he thinks, want not/waste not! He's likely to get a small amount bidding through his invite-only open market connection.

Humming again, but louder now. The next step is preserving the pancreas, then corneas, finally ending with the heart—again, none of which are on the client list.

He finishes both extraction and packing in under twenty-three minutes. This is a personal best, but there is no one to share it with.

Thus begins the cleanup.

Alexei wipes each instrument, deposits it in a ziplock for disposal, and peels off his gloves with a practiced flick. He layers the coolers with ice packs and insulating foam, then labels each with tissue type, time, and a code only the buyer will recognize. The dining room, once so pristine, now looks like a crime scene staged by a perfectionist. He wraps the corpse like a mummy—one layer, then another, with a final cocoon of black trash bags. He surveys the rest, then peels the tape from the baseboards and bundles the plastic, folding it inward to contain the splatter.

He maneuvers the package through the kitchen to the back stairs. After opening the door, he steps onto the porch, and inhales the taste of winter. The air is glass-clear, but edged with the distant burn of wood smoke. He descends the steps, boots creaking on the frost-slick wood, and loads the coolers into the bed of the pickup, beneath a tarp.

After he arranges the valuable trove of cargo, he returns to heft up the disposable portion. That's when this unfamiliar sensation pricks at his scalp: an uncanny certainty of being watched. He holds still, not breathing, and scans the tree line, the roofline, the empty road beyond. There is nothing there—no cars, no movement, not even the usual deer that haunt the ditches after dusk.

Alexei remains motionless for several heartbeats, the plastic-wrapped corpse balanced on his shoulder, the world holding its breath.

The sensation fades, replaced by a low, involuntary shiver. He shrugs, tosses the body into the truck bed, and latches the tailgate.

The delivery is in six hours, and he is the Deliverer. He has ninety minutes to clean the house, change clothes, and drive north to the drop point.

He lingers on the porch, head tilted, listening for any sensation again. The only noise is the whine of the furnace kicking on inside. He glances upward: the stars are hidden, the sky a seamless wool blanket, nothing watching but the cold.

Returning to the kitchen, Alexei washes his hands until they are pink and raw, then pours himself a shot of cheap vodka. He downs it, neat, not savoring the burn.

He sits at the kitchen table, staring at the last cooler by the door, and allows himself a minute to simply exist. There is no guilt, no regret, no emotion at all. Just the afterglow of a job done perfectly.

Somewhere in the distance, a dog barks.

He finishes a second shot of vodka, puts on a clean shirt, and moves to the truck. The night accepts him, and the world resumes its silence. As it should.

Chapter One

Should be Glad

From the plank sign, warped and half-legible in the Appalachian fog, Evie could tell this isn't a bar with a regular clientele so much as a holding pond for the displaced, and the briefly unsupervised. A weathered brewery logo from the eighties flanks the door. The inside air sits humid with fryer oil, but the floor gleams shockingly clean—either the staff do care or the patrons are fewer and less lively than expected.

The Rusty Nail's interior runs narrow and deep, with four tall tables by the window and a twelve-seat bar top stretching along the wall. She counts: one old-timer with a newspaper, two late-shift miners in reflective bibs, and a studious gal wearing noise-canceling headphones and nursing an umbrella drink. The male bartender, hair the color of gunpowder, meets her eyes with that small-town blend of curiosity and suspicion. He nods.

She drops onto a stool at the farthest end. Evie orders a double whiskey—no ice, no garnish, no brand preference. The bartender pours something viscous and honey-brown, slides the glass over a cocktail napkin, then withdraws.

Her hands look steadier than she feels. Evie's nerves have been humming since yesterday morning, when a news alert pinged about a "possible ViCAP-related double homicide" in a county two hours from her old home. She guesses the old bureaucracy has left her privileged access open still. These notifications will fade away before too long once they get the resignation memo.

Evie's whiskey sip flows down, burning her fatigue into submission. She closes her eyes for a beat, then forces them open. The memory of her last, lost case, as well as her daughter-shaped hole presses at the back of her skull. Without practiced precision and routine as her crutch, the relentless murmur of the bar's TV disrupts her means of coping. The sound is a persistent thrum. It loops through high-school basketball scores, making it challenging to keep those painful memories of her late daughter at bay.

She is on her second glass and the first fries of the evening when she feels the of attention of bar shift. The old-timer is gone; the two miners have merged into a single slumped silhouette. That just leaves the student, herself, and the bartender remaining. He stacks pint glasses with the brittle focus of someone trying not to eavesdrop.

Then someone of beefier stock enters The Nail. Large, meaty, thirty or forty, beard trimmed but going salt-and-pepper at the chin. Flannel two sizes too tight; Carhartt vest; and boots truly abused. He surveys the space with the wide swing of a man used to being observed, then makes for the bar.

Mr. Beef takes the stool beside hers, though eight other options remain.

Evie restrains her eye roll, intent on the plate before her. She angles her body a degree farther away and returns to her fries. The man flags the bartender, orders a Bud and a bourbon shot, and turns his whole body toward her in the universal language of 'I am here for interaction, and I do not fear rejection.'

"Evenin'," he says, letting the word hang. He gives her a long, evaluating look. "Don't get too many fillies like you around here. Just passin' through?"

Debating the optimal response, Evie calculates the risk of candor, selects the safest lie. "Just aiming for a sip and some solitude. On my way to a funeral."

He lets out a short laugh, as if it were a joke in a foreign tongue. "Not the best reason for a trip, but I hear the dead can be a comfort." He pronounces 'comfort' as two distinct syllables.

"Whiskey's cheaper than grief counseling," she replies.

He snorts and smiles, unveiling a chipped canine.

His forearms get her attention first: corded muscle, river-delta of scar tissue across his right hand. Manual labor, probably local, something with heavy machinery. They're too clean to be mechanics, so maybe construction or the gas company. She catalogs the rest: cheap deodorant overlaying deeper notes of smoke and oil, a nervous leg bounce under the bar, a tendency to inhale before he speaks as if bracing for an incoming punch.

"You got family?" he says, gesturing with his bottle. "Or just the dead ones?"

She bristles. "No."

He doesn't hear her intent and just steps over it. "That's a goddamn shame. A woman alone is a mighty choice around here. Not sayin' you can't handle yourself, just—" He mimes a fistfight with the air, then shrugs.

Evie clocks his eyes. They flick up and down her frame, maybe assessing for anything concealed. He won't find either, at least not pepper spray. She sips again, lets the silence yawn open, hopes the others present might dissuade further escalation. The student, however, retreats further behind her headphones.

He tries again. "I could keep you company, if ya ask nice. Or if you're more a 'leave-me-alone' type, I can do that too." He gives a performative little bow.

She stares at his reflection in the bar mirror. "I'm fine on my own."

He raises his hands. "Hey, no worries. Just lookin' out for a neighbor, you know?"

She lets her mouth settle into a line. "You don't know me."

He leans in, lowering his voice. "I could, if ya want."

The bartender drops by, gives Evie a look of mute apology, and places her next whiskey within easy reach. Mr. Beef watches the transaction, then turns his attention back to her with a glimmer of challenge in his eyes.

"You know, I used to do some security work. Bars like this, you gotta have someone keep the peace. Not sayin' you need it, but—" He gestures again, flexing his arm.

Her inner profiler registers the micro-expressions: half-second tightening at the jaw, dilation of pupils, the way he smiles only with his mouth, never the eyes. A man accustomed to getting what he wants, or at least never punished for trying.

He tries a new tack. "You got a name?"

"Evie."

He rolls it around in his mouth. "Pretty. Mine's Greg. So, Evie—what's your thing? Besides funerals."

She wants to say 'homicide' just to watch his reaction, but instead shrugs. "I'm between things."

He smiles, sensing a possible in. "Hey, we all are. Between jobs, between wives, between paychecks." Greg snorts. "Sometimes between jail sentences, but that's just this part of the country."

Evie lets her silence answer.

He gulps his bourbon, motions for another. "You sure you're good here? Lotta weirdos roll through after dark. This bar's the only one for fifteen miles, you know."

She taps her empty glass—signaling she's had enough.

He sees it. "How about I walk you to your car? Don't need to talk or anything, just—escort."

She looks at his hands, open and loose on the bar. She pictures the scenario: he follows her out, tries to herd her toward the lot, maybe hopes for a little resistance to sweeten the pursuit. He's not here for conversation.

Evie sets her money on the bar, with an extra fiver for the bartender, and stands. He rises with her, all eager gallantry. "Let's go," he says, as if already decided.

She walks to the door, keeping her pace measured, every sense peeled open for the lunge that might come at any moment. In the glass, she catches the student's eyes following her, wide and unblinking, as if watching a live-animal documentary. The bartender doesn't look up.

Cold air hits her face as she pushes open the door. Evie tugs her jacket closer. The man follows. He says nothing, but his boot falls land in perfect rhythm with her own.

She turns left toward the side street and the orange halo of her motel sign. The road lies deserted, muffled by a dusting of fresh snow and an underlying threat of ice. Shoulders square, Evie walks. He keeps pace behind her, saying nothing, letting the silence grow into a dare.

At the first corner, he speaks again, low and friendly, as if to a frightened animal. "You know, you don't have to act tough. I could—"

She cuts him off with a look. "You could what?"

He blinks, thrown by the interruption. "Help is all. Some of these back roads aren't safe for a... Someone alone."

She pauses under the streetlight. "I'm not alone."

He laughs, but it comes stilted. "Yeah, okay."

Not responding, she lets him see her face, all lines and shadows and none of the fear he's mining for. Then she walks on, entering the motel parking lot. She's already got a room. But her car is three paces ahead. The office, dark and empty, is just off to the side. Mr. Beef—Greg—quickens his approach in a way that will intersect just shy of her driver's-side door.

She turns again, just enough to register his silhouette against the streetlamp. He isn't smiling now. His face sets, calculating.

"You got something to say, say it," she tells him, voice level.

Greg stops, but not out of deference—just in the mental arithmetic of predator and prey. He shakes his head, half-laughs. "It's funny. You act tough, but out here? Alone? That's not smart." He looks at her, really looks, his eyes crawling over her again.

She reaches for the car handle. The alarm chirps as she pulls. He closes the distance—too fast, too close. Beef's hand clamps her forearm. She feels the warmth of his palm even through the coat; the pressure calibrated below the threshold of injury.

Evie sighs. "This will not end well for you."

He leans in, breath a mix of whiskey and bile. "Some folk need to be learnt the hard way," he says, and his hand tightens.

It happens without conscious intent. The trauma, the unvoiced rage—all of that hovers in the background. What emerges, sharp and clean, is the other thing, the presence she feels when no one is around. It's like a voltage spike, a bounce of the room's air pressure, a small darkness that accumulates behind her eyes and shrinks the world to a single point of attention.

She leers up at him.

Even in the night, he sees the change. His grip falters. He flinches at her black stare. But then, she's so tiny to him. Reasserting himself, Greg crowds. "C'mon, this'll be good for ya."

Evie places her left hand atop his grip. Like an arctic breeze, cold flows through her into him. Greg shudders with the sour chill of someone peeing on his grave. His jaw hangs slack, eyes widen. Then casually, Evie reaches into her jacket and pulls the Glock from its holster. She slides it under his ribcage, and presses.

He freezes. Every blood vessel in his body appears to contract.

Waiting a half-beat, Evie lets him taste the consequence. "A dumb-ass lout like you should be glad a girl like me doesn't need the legal hassles," she says, cold and certain. "Next time you put your hands on someone, I hope they're not as patient as this filly."

He tries to speak, but it comes out as a gulp.

She shoves. Not hard, just enough to cue the distance. He stumbles, blanches, nearly slips on ice, and for a second she thinks he might actually piss himself. He doesn't, but she wouldn't bet against there being an added dampening of his drawers.

Holstering the weapon, Evie turns toward her motel door. She opens it and watches him stagger back to the bar. His shoulders are hunched, one hand cupping his ribs as if the bullet is already inside him.

With the closing of the latch, she lets out a sigh and discovers the full-length mirror behind the door. For several seconds she just stands there, staring at her own eyes in the reflection. The darkness, the absence of the whites... They still don't blink enough, but then they've seen so much already.

Chapter Two

Intersections

Ohio in late November is a world sheared down to its essentials: azure sky, blunt fields, and the handwriting of bare trees along the horizon. The old Ford Fiesta holds just enough heat to fog the inside glass, so Evie cracks the window. She dials the defrost and guides the little car through a vein of two-lane county highways, passing barns that look abandoned even when they're not. The West Virginia foothills are behind her now; the land flattens out as she heads west, chewing through forty miles of frost-scorched soybean and corn stubble.

The radio is off—Evie prefers her own head noise to the morning chatter. Besides, nothing on the dial would improve this mood. The previous night's echo—a near-assault in a motel parking lot, the old temptations licking at her teeth—keeps replaying itself in new edits. By the fifth or sixth loop, she's already sick of herself.

She stops at a gas station that boasts fresh donuts and two-for-three roller dogs. Evie grabs a black coffee, ignores the sugar, and stands near the entryway a moment, taking in the rural morning. A pair of retirees argue over lottery tickets at the counter. A mother herds three kids through the automatic doors, their boots slapping on the tile in rhythm. One of them stares at her—the oldest girl, maybe eight—with open curiosity. It takes Evie a half-second to realize she's still in her night-black shirt, the one with the FBI logo she told herself she'd stop wearing once she quit. She tugs her coat closed and pays in cash, offering the clerk her most generic smile.

Back on the road, caffeine steadily works its way into her bloodstream.

The car groans over a rutted railroad crossing and descends into the outer orbit of what passes for a city here. Bank, pharmacy, a new Dollar General, then Main Street proper. She's early, so she lets herself idle through a few blocks, reading the faces of the people on the sidewalks, counting how many are bundled against the cold and how many just accept it like a chronic pain. The town is prepping for Christmas already: windows painted with canned-snow, old garland strung between lamp posts. There is not a speck of actual snow illuminated by the daylight.

At a four-way intersection, the light flips red, and Evie's car idles. Two SUVs and a rusted-out Tacoma line up behind her; ahead, a parade of pedestrians waits for the walk signal. She drums her fingers on the steering wheel.

She notes the crossing crowd in profiler's shorthand: the pack of high schoolers, oversized parkas and identical slouching; a woman with a double stroller, face set in the pained neutrality of all mothers everywhere; an older man in a battered VFW cap, shuffle-stepping across the frostbit crosswalk.

And one woman who doesn't fit.

Evie clocks her immediately: mid-twenties, tall and slender, with a posture not ruined by screens or manual labor. She's not moving, not talking, just standing at the curb with her hands folded over her stomach. Her blouse is half-unbuttoned, despite the temperature, and there's a mottled stain of red, dark and stiffening, from the collarbone down. Flaxen hair flutters in the wind, covering most of her face. No coat, not even a jacket. Nobody else seems to notice her.

The light changes. Evie slowly rolls forward, craning herself to hold the view as the woman remains rooted. Evie doesn't even flinch at the horn's blare behind her. At the midpoint of the intersection, the blonde woman lifts her head.

Through the driver-side window, they make eye contact. Evie can't explain the mathematics of it—how a look can pass through a dozen yards of country air, through a moving car, through the ordinary haze of the day—but it does. The woman's face is gray as candle wax; her eyes are deep-threaded with distant, starlike pinpricks. For a half-beat, the entire tableau freezes: Evie's grip tightens on the wheel, the blood on the woman's shirt stark as paint.

Then, as if tugged by an invisible wire, the woman jerks forward. She steps out, not onto the crosswalk, but into oncoming traffic. A barreling tractor trailer plows toward her, as if the driver doesn't even know she's there.

It's too surreal. That can't be. She's a—

Evie stomps on the brake. The car behind her lies on the horn, the sound so loud it blows out every other sense.

There is no impact. Instead, as the tractor trailer passes, the woman is just—gone. Not dodged, not sprinted, not flattened against the pavement. There's nothing but empty air and a drift of dry leaves swirling in the semi's slipstream.

Evie sits there, both feet hard on the brake, as the SUV behind her leans on its horn again. She twists to look in the mirror, expecting chaos or at least a mess of pedestrians scattered like bowling pins, but the crosswalk is normal. That VFW man shuffles on. The mother adjusts her stroller, yanking the smallest child back from the curb. The high schoolers have already reached the opposite side and are retreating into the donut shop. No sign of the woman, no bloody blouse, nothing out of place except the hairline fracture of cold running up Evie's spine.

The SUV pulls around her, the driver—red-faced, pork-chop mustache—screaming something out the window. She can't hear it over the thunder in her own chest.

The light is still green. Evie releases the brake and coasts, slow, as if expecting the next second to explode.

She makes the next right and parks in the shade of a tree. Breath comes shallow and high in her chest, as if she's been running a mile. She kills the engine and sits with her hands in her lap. The rationalist in her does its best. Stress, fatigue, PTSD, a trick of the light. She runs herself through the checklist: medications, sleep debt, last meal. All plausible. All inadequate.

It's only been a day since she left Quantico. Should she be surprised this might happen so soon? Evie knows what she saw.

She opens the glove compartment, fishes out the cheap plastic bottle she keeps for emergencies. The label's worn, but she recognizes the clatter of the pills inside by sound alone. She pours two antacids into her palm, chew-swallows, and waits for the chalky aftertaste to fade.

Outside, the town keeps moving, unbothered by the apparition that just rewrote her morning.

She catches herself checking the mirror, just to be sure the woman isn't reflected there, grinning or reaching through the glass. Nothing but her own brown eyes, bloodshot now, the lines at the corners deepening.

"A ghost," she mutters. "Just great. Guess this is a thing now."

She sits for a few minutes more, counting down the beats until her pulse flattens. It's still more than an hour away from Hillsboro. She wonders if it will be as easy to ignore what's happening to her with her devoted parents present.

Evie restarts the car, lets the engine idle, and merges back into the slow river of traffic. At the next intersection, she checks every face in the crosswalk, but the bloody woman is nowhere to be found.

Still, for the rest of the morning, every time Evie blinks, there are those starlit eyes burned into her replay.

Chapter Three

Homecoming and Hard Truths

The house is almost exactly as she remembers it, which isn't the same as unchanged. A little more siding chipped off the gutters; the flag on the porch was now replaced with a "Blessed" sign from one of those internet shops; new LED bulbs in the front fixtures, more blue compared to the old sodium glow. The lawn is patchy, the grass gone over to straw, but the rhododendrons by the steps are pruned—her father's handiwork. There's a faint scent of wood smoke, which means her mother is using the fireplace.

Evie pulls her overnight bag from the back seat, double-checks that her laptop is zipped away, and scans the front windows. Two familiar figures: one larger, head stooped, hands in pockets; the other shorter, close-cropped hair, arms crossed in anticipation. The screen door opens. She gives herself two full breaths before walking up the drive.

Mom meets her on the patio, wearing a holiday sweater. Carol Whitaker is still barely five feet, still built like a former gymnast hiding from her own muscle memory. She wraps Evie in a hug that's all restraint at first, then tightens at the last moment so hard it pops something in Evie's upper back.

"Baby girl," Mom says, rocking her side to side. "You made it! Oh, look at you—thin as a rail. When was your last proper meal?"

"That'd be a judgement call," Evie says, muffled in the cardigan. She gets a hand around her mother's shoulders and squeezes back. "Might've been a while."

Henry Cross, Dad, appears in the doorway. He's still tall, but something in his shape has gone more pear than tree trunk. He gives Evie a one-armed hug, then claps her on the back. She feels the gesture as a release—of tension, of expectation.

"You made good time," Dad says. "Roads weren't bad?"

"Just cold. Fog in the valleys," Evie says.

Mom grabs her bag before she can object and ushers her into the foyer, a corridor of family photos and greeting cards taped to the wall. Inside, it smells of coffee and bread—her mother has clearly stress-baked in advance.

"Sit. You must be exhausted," Mom says, aiming Evie for the couch. She hesitates, caught by the nostalgia of the living room: the old sofa, the hand-knitted afghan, the same end table from the year Evie left for Quantico. There's even the old TV, flat-screen but ancient in electronics years, displaying a news channel with the sound muted.

Mom parks herself on the edge of an armchair and starts wringing her hands. Dad lingers behind, half in the hallway.

"You want coffee, honey?" she asks. "Or something stronger?"

Evie almost confronts him with, I'm sober, but bites it back. "Coffee's always good. Thanks."

As Mom departs to the kitchen, Dad settles onto the edge of the couch. He studies her face, lips pursed. "You okay?" he asks, keeping his voice low.

Evie nods. "Just tired. It's just been... quite a week."

He nods, like he's in on some secret suffering. "You staying long?"

"Not sure yet. Got some things on my mind. Slow progress working through."

He gauges her for a moment, then leans in. "Your mom's worried. She says you sound different on the phone."

Evie shrugs. "Hard to be upbeat these days."

He grunts in agreement and turns his attention to the TV. For half a minute, neither of them says anything. The kitchen sounds—ceramic from the cabinet, pouring coffee—punctuate the silence.

Carol returns with the mug; cream slowly swirls. She hands it to Evie, then sits again, perching like a bird about to take flight.

"So," Mom says, folding her hands in her lap, "are you ready to talk?"

"About?" Evie asks.

"About what you're doing next; the job, your house, Michael, everything." Mom's eyes are a little too bright. "This limbo can't last forever."

Evie taps the rim of her mug with a fingertip. "I signed the papers last week. Michael is handling the agent. Half the money will come to me whenever it sells. I don't want the furniture, or the dishes, or anything else."

Henry grunts. "Too bad. Still wanted to believe you two could work it out."

"And the job?" Carol's voice is soft, but the edge is there.

Evie keeps her eyes on the coffee. "I'm on leave, effective two days ago. Probation technically, but I don't expect to go back." She waits for the reaction.

Her mother's jaw works in micro-spasms, but she keeps it together. "That's... a lot," she says. "After all you've put into it."

Evie shrugs. "Things change."

Dad tries to rescue the mood. "Hell, you always said retirement was just an invitation for arthritis. Maybe you can take a vacation. Visit some beach somewheres."

Mom shoots him a look, then returns to Evie. "You're not just doing this for Michael, are you?" she asks, voice hushed.

Evie laughs, but it's hollow. "Michael is the least of my problems."

The silence thickens, then Mom softens her tone. "You told me on the phone there were... signs. That you needed to come home, listen for direction." She leans forward. "I'm not trying to badger you, but this isn't like you, Evie. You never talk much about faith."

Evie's throat tightens. She doesn't want this conversation, but it was coming.

"I just..." She pauses. The right words don't exist. She settles on the closest tale to the truth. "It feels like I need to listen for once. Not just... act."

Dad tilts his head. "Listen to whom?"

Evie's head drifts, eyes focused on nothing in particular. "To God. Or whatever's left of Him."

Mom's hands fly to her chest. "Oh, Evie, we've always hoped you'd find some understanding. For you to come back to..." She stops, as if sensing the boundary.

Evie shakes her head. "I'm not coming back to anything. I just—there's something I need to figure out, and I don't want to do it anywhere near D.C. That's all."

Henry nods, like he's seen this show. "You know, your grandfather said the same thing once. Just up and left his job, said the Lord would show him what was next."

"And did He?" Evie's lip quirks.

"He started a worm farm," Dad says, deadpan.

Mom slaps his arm. "It paid the bills," she mutters.

Evie snorts. The tension recedes a hair.

Her mother seizes the opening. "If you're truly searching, I want you to consider coming to service on Sunday. Just to sit. No pressure. Pastor Rachel's doing a series on spiritual warfare and—" she cuts herself off again, eyes darting to Evie's reaction.

Evie forces a polite smile. "That sounds nice."

They let it drop for a minute. Dad shifts his weight, glances at the muted news. "How about joining your old dad? Not much on the tube," he says, but it's clear he doesn't care what's on.

Evie nods, grateful for the distraction. "Sure. As long as it's not cable news."

He flips to the game show channel, where an episode of Wheel of Fortune is in progress. The host's smile is the same as always: a little too practiced, a little too perfect. They watch in silence, Evie sipping her coffee, Mom fussing with a loose thread on her sweater. The contestant misses the puzzle. Dad laughs, low and appreciative, and even Evie grins at the simplicity of it all.

When the first commercial hits, Mom turns to Evie, voice gentle. "I know you're hurting," she says. "I wish I could fix it."

Evie looks off. "I wish you could too."

Moving to the couch, Mom sits beside her, and wraps her hand around Evie's. The gesture is warm, familiar, and just tight enough to be a promise. "I'm glad you're home," she says.

Evie nods, unable to speak.

They watch the next round in silence; the letters flipping over one by one, the answer more obvious with each guess. Evie feels her own puzzle pieces sliding into place: not hopeful, but at least honest.

When the show ends, Dad stands, pats his thigh, and says, "I'll get your room ready."

Mom leans against Evie's shoulder. "We kept it just like you left it."

Evie smiles, because that's certainly a half-truth.

Intercepting Evie at the foot of the stairs, Mom has a towel bundle in one arm, spare sheets tucked under the other. She's moved from the emotional to the practical in record time.

"You remember where it is," Mom says, leading Evie up the creaking staircase. "But I swapped out the curtains for blackout ones, since your dad's on that new shift and needs his sleep during the day. Hope that's okay."

"Blackout is perfect," Evie says, one hand on the banister. The wood feels less polished than she remembers—tiny ridges have surfaced.

Mom pushes open the guest room door. The air inside is a degree cooler than the hallway, and it has the particular scent of disuse: dust, cedar, the echo of last winter's chill.

"We didn't change much," Mom says, laying the towels at the foot of the bed. "Well, I did move your trophies to the shelf, so they wouldn't get knocked over when I vacuumed."

Evie sets her bag down on the faded rug and surveys the space. A narrow twin bed, iron frame, the old quilt she used as a child. The shelf is crowded with relics: her high school valedictorian plaque, the Psych Olympiad medal, a photo of her in Quantico class blues. Above the headboard hangs the cross—wooden, smooth, barely the size of her palm. There's a bookshelf by the window, filled with psych journals and textbooks, all marked with neon flags and penciled notes. On the desk sits a dog-shaped lamp, its shade still wrapped in a plastic sleeve. Everything has the look of careful preservation, as if her departure at eighteen was a temporary leave.

Mom straightens the quilt, her hand lingering a second too long on the pillow. "I put on fresh sheets, and if you need the space heater, it's in the closet. Your dad refuses to turn up the thermostat until Christmas." She smiles, soft around the eyes. "There's a new bottle of shampoo in the bathroom, too. That kind you liked."

Evie nods. "Thanks, Mom."

Mom folds her hands, like she's suppressing more words. "I know you don't want to talk tonight, but if you ever do... we're just down the hall."

Evie nods again, sharper this time. "I know. I'll be fine."

"I mean it," she says. "I prayed for this day, but I wasn't expecting it to feel..." She stops herself, then smiles, covering the crack. "Well, good night, honey."

Evie waits for the footsteps to fade before she moves. She unzips her bag, removes her laptop, charger, rolls off the rosaries from her wrist, and places them with the Glock in the top drawer of the nightstand. The act is so practiced it's muscle memory. She pulls out a clean shirt, hangs it on the closet hook, and lines her shoes up by the door—right foot first, left a half-inch ahead, routine to the rescue.

She sits at the desk and powers on the laptop. The blackout curtains have muted the world outside, so only the thinnest outline of sun seeps around the edges. The room is soon an island in a dim ocean; her face lit in electric blue.

Evie opens her browser, fingers hovering over the keyboard. The first search is mechanical: Alexander Mercer.

The autofill suggests "Alexander Mercer net worth," "Alexander Mercer scandal," "Alexander Mercer dead." She ignores them, types in "Alexander Mercer Global Enterprises" and reads the top hits.

The man is everywhere. There are news articles about his philanthropy, exposes about alleged tax evasion, and a few clickbait stories about his "mysterious illness." Photos show him attending galas, at UN conferences, shaking hands with prime ministers. Always the same tight-lipped smile, eyes that never quite meet the camera.

She scans his biography. Born in Indiana, but relocated to Switzerland as a teen. Tech prodigy, two doctorates, founded his own data company at twenty-one. There are rumors of connections to the defense industry, but nothing proven. Married three times, four children. Known to fund art installations, brain research, and several midwestern politicians. There's a section about his recent "health struggles"—Mercer has not appeared in public for six months, but his company insists he's still at the helm.

Evie opens the next dozen links, skimming for patterns. She doesn't find much, but she notes that every photo of Mercer is either old or heavily staged. None of the recent images match the candids from public appearances a few years ago. His face has changed—gaunter, paler, eyes slightly recessed. There's a harshness to his features that reminds her of the ghost in the crosswalk.

She bookmarks the articles, makes a folder called MERCER, and starts a spreadsheet with dates and locations. Every new data point tightens her focus, like a camera lens narrowing the depth of field.

As she types, the dark settles deeper into the room. Her parents are voices downstairs, muffled by drywall and distance. A TV chatters low.

The furnace clicks on, blowing a brief heat that tinges of disuse. Guess Mom convinced him to do otherwise.

Evie returns to the spreadsheet, tracking Mercer's last confirmed sighting: a conference in Zurich, nearly eight months ago. Since then, there have been only rumors and planted press releases. She feels the old profiler's itch, the sense of a pattern just out of sight. She clicks through another dozen articles, searching for the connective tissue.

Outside, the wind stirs against the house. As the sun sets, the world becomes smaller, more manageable.

She looks up at the cross over her bed, then back at Mercer's face. "You're next," she says, voice barely above a whisper.

Closing the laptop, she plunges the room into utter black.

Chapter Four

Unseen Patterns

There's no waking ahead of country parents. And Evie is quite content getting up well after sunrise, though one couldn't tell by the blackout curtains. She peels them back, letting in the November sun. Her phone says 9:11 AM.

She wasn't a morning person, even in childhood. Dawns were spent hoarding the silence before school—reading her way through a hundred mysteries, or simply staring at the ceiling and mapping her life in the future tense. Now, the routine is different: open laptop, inventory the overnight news cycle, sweep for movement in the world of her target.

Evie pulls the desk chair close, sets her coffee beside the trackpad, and powers up. Her machine is somewhat old, the keys worn shiny by years of angry report-writing and late-night database mining. She logs in with an alias, better not to draw attention to herself, plus because learned habits never truly die.

There is a reply waiting in her alias inbox. Subject: MERCER. She clicks. The message is just two lines:

- Rumors of ill health—media controlled blackout

- No public events for 79 days (Zurich incident)

She reads it twice. Her hacker contacts usually elaborate, so even these few words mean more than they say. The "media blackout" tells her Mercer's people have gone into siege mode, controlling information at the source. The "Zurich incident" is new, and the number—seventy-nine days—means someone's clocking his movements in real time.

She minimizes the email and pulls up her spreadsheet. Each cell is a microcosm: dates, venues, timestamps, who appeared on stage with Mercer, who shook his hand, who looked uncomfortable doing it. Updating the Zurich entry, she bolds the date of last sighting.

Evie has spent her career deconstructing motives. The shape of a killer's mind is rarely a mystery to her. What keeps her up at night is the way certain patterns echo: how the rich and the predatory build concentric rings of protection, how their public faces are curated to the point of unreality. It's the same with Mercer, but his scale is off the charts. He isn't just an oligarch; he's a case study in profiting from entropy.

She opens another tab and starts hunting through the usual leaks and back channels. The routine is soothing—one part profiler, one part forensic accountant. Each headline is a data point. Each photograph is a vector. The high-resolution images show Mercer at conferences, flanked by aides, always upright, always crisp-suited. But in the last year, something is changing in the posture, the angle of the jaw. He's shrinking. Pale, drawn, sometimes sporting a scarf or turtleneck even in summer.

She starts a folder: HEALTH.

There's another layer, one that would interest her mother if she could ever bring herself to share it. The occult details. Mercer has funded at least three research projects on "non-local consciousness." He gave an endowment to a university lab shut down for ethical violations—victims were described as "cognitively exacerbated." And in every city where the Cartographer staged a victim, there's a shell company registered to a trust with one of Mercer's lawyers on the letterhead.

Evie's mouth goes dry as she lines up the data.

She clicks through to a dark web aggregator. The search string is precise: "Mercer + Cartographer + disappearance." There are a few hits, most garbage, but one thread jumps out: a forum post from an account called NEWJERICHO, dated the day after her daughter vanished.

- Found another one. Target moved. Revert to control.

Evie copies the text into her notes. The language is familiar—it mirrors the serial killer's diction, but refracted through a new lens. It reads more like an internal memo than a taunt. The last phrase: revert to control.

She tries not to interpret it.

Her eyes drift to the window, to the bare tangle of trees outside. She remembers how her daughter used to race around the backyard, coatless and oblivious to the cold, her laughter bouncing between fences. The memory lands on her chest like a rock. She pushes it away and returns to the screen.

She checks her cellphone. The battery is at 62%. There are no missed calls, no messages. No threats. But then, genuine threats never announce themselves. They simply show up and rewire your life.

Evie paces the length of her childhood bedroom. There's the Psych Olympiad medal, the photograph of her in class blues. She wonders if the girl in the photo would recognize the person standing here now.

She sits and writes a single line at the top of a fresh document:

THEORY: What if Mercer is dying?

She lists out the evidence:

- Absence from public view
- Documented health decline (photographic only)
- Increased research into consciousness, mind transfer
- Victims match prior escalation pattern
- Shell companies linked to Cartographer killings

Evie spends the morning collecting datasets. Winnowing her way through various inconsequential corporate restructurings and acquisitions. By the time the sun reaches its midday southern zenith, it throws a pale halo around the cross on her wall. For a second, Evie almost laughs. She wonders if even God is interested in what's coming. Who knows? Maybe she's part of his plan.

Somewhere in her yesterday thoughts there is a cold echo of that woman's eyes—star-punctured, hollow, infinitely awake—watching her from a busy street corner.

She stands and stretches, shaking out her arms.

That's when her mother summons. When Carol Whitaker hollers up the stairwell, the sound punches through the wall like a brick. "Lunch is ready, and your dad's home!"

It's not a request.

Evie shoves her notes and phone beneath a folder labeled "Insurance," slaps the laptop lid closed, and stands. Her left leg is numb from being cross-legged too long; she hobbles the first step, then forces herself into a normal stride. The air in the hallway is warmer, scented with bread and the faintest hint of Lysol.

The kitchen has not changed: square linoleum tiles, gold-flecked formica, the fridge plastered with expired coupons and church retreat magnets. Dad is at the table, forearms darkened and rough from a morning of building ramps for the local Habitat for Humanity. His hair, always buzzed high and tight, now grows wild at the temples—unruly steel gray. He grins at Evie, sawdust grit still in his knuckles.

"Hey, Superstar," he says. "You saving the world today, or just your own headspace?"

Evie mumbles a greeting and slides into her old seat.

Mom sets a plate in front of Evie: tuna sandwich, carrot sticks, potato chips. The food is retrograde, the kind her mother made every Saturday. Mom sits down after, smoothing her apron.

The TV over the sink hums with the background noise of a conservative news station. Sound low, closed captions scrolling. Dad spies on it between bites. For a minute, the scene is so normal it almost feels like a contemporary Rockwell painting.

Henry gestures at the news crawl. "You see this thing in Missouri? People are nuts."

Evie shrugs, eyeing the captions. "I've been off the grid. What thing?"

Carol answers, her voice feather-light: "It's a murder. Out near St. Louis. Some poor man just vanished, and now the police found... well, it doesn't bear repeating at the table."

Dad chews, swallows. "I'll repeat it—these cults seem like they're everywhere now. Damned devil worship."

Evie's mind snaps into a familiar gear. "'Vanished,' you say?"

Mom nods. "It's the strangest part. I read in the paper, police found his car abandoned. It's like he just got out and walked away. Then the body turned up later."

Dad grunts. "Cops always say that, even when it's drugs or gambling or who knows. The world's gone crazy."

The TV shows a photograph: a smiling man, late-twenties, athletic, shoulder-to-shoulder with volleyball teammates. Below the caption: "Local man missing since Tuesday. Found dead in Cuivre River State Park." The anchor's lips move in slow motion. Evie reads: "Authorities have no current leads... No signs of struggle... If you have any information, no matter how small, you are urged to contact CrimeStoppers at..."

She can't help herself. "No suspects?"

Dad shakes his head. "Not likely. If not Satanists, then it's some meth tweaker."

Mom makes a noise, halfway between a sigh and a prayer. "It's just so sad. Reminds me of the Janes girl a few months back, the one by the lake. What's happening in the world, Evie?"

Evie has no answer that wouldn't terrify them. She chews her sandwich and watches the TV, irresistibly scanning for anomalies: mismatched numbers, odd turns of phrase. But everything in the report is routine.

Her parents lapse into silence, both looking at her, as if she might break the code. In a way, she knows they expect her to. The prodigal profiler back in town. It's what they tell people at church.

Evie tries to smile. "Sometimes people just snap," she says. "Doesn't mean it's a pattern."

Dad gives her a look—half admiration, half skepticism. "You always were the logical one."

Mom softens. "Forgive me, dear. I know the FBI was important to you, but part of me is just glad you will not be mixed up in these things anymore."

The silence hangs. The TV flips to commercial. A Medicare ad: an old man hugs a happy grandson, then morphs to a worried woman counting pills at her kitchen table. The cycle repeats.

Evie drinks her water.

She opens her mouth to excuse herself, but catches a flicker of movement beyond the window. In the backyard, a squirrel scurries up a tree, its bushy tail flicking as it nibbles on an acorn. The midday sky is clear; all the clouds burned away. Beyond the patio, at the fence line, a figure stands. Evie's brain tries to overlay sense onto it: neighbor? delivery? But it's neither.

It is a young woman, blonde hair tossing in the wind. Her blouse is all too familiar. Though she is facing away from the house, Evie knows instantly it's the same as before—the woman from the crosswalk, the vision that haunted her on the country drive in. The one with the bloodstained collar.

She begins to pivot, as if spun by the breeze in slow motion.

Evie goes ice-cold. She stands, tips her chair, and bolts for the back door.

Dad barks, "Evie?" but she doesn't stop.

She yanks open the sliding glass, and the November air assaults her: hard, metallic, edged with a coming snow. By the time she crosses the threshold and sprints onto the patio, bare feet on the cement, the spirit is gone.

For three full seconds, she stands there, panting, fists balled. Then, from inside, her mother calls—a note Evie's never heard before.

She turns away from the patio, back into the kitchen warmth. Mom and Dad are standing before the table, faces pale, eyes wide as teacups.

Evie slides the door closed. No one speaks.

Finally, Mom finds her voice: "Evie, what on earth?"

Evie tries to find an answer. None of them fit. "I thought I saw... someone."

Dad's eyes bore into her. "You sure you're okay?"

She nods. "It was nothing."

The word hangs in the air like a lie.

Her parents look at each other, the way people do when they're recalibrating expectations. It's a silent communication, loaded with concern. Dad shrugs.

Thus, lunch resumes. The sandwich has gone soft; the carrots sweat condensation onto the plate. The TV blares a new story, some congressional hearing, but no one is watching.

Evie sits and finishes her meal, every sense tuned to the window behind her. She can still see the spot where the woman stood, the faintest imprint, like sunburn, on the edge of her vision.

Mom clears her throat. "You know, maybe a nap might do you good, Evie. Or maybe a walk with me later?"

She nods, not trusting herself to say anything.

Her father reaches over, rests his palm on her hand. "We're glad you're home, you know that? Whatever's going on, we'll figure it out."

Evie's jaw tightens, but she forces a smile. "I know. Thanks, Dad."

After lunch, she carries her plate to the sink, stacks it on top of a pink plastic cup, and turns on the faucet. The water runs ice-cold, biting her hands.

She dries her fingers, peeks once more out the window, and heads back up the stairs.

Chapter Five

Yours to Carry

The stairs are cooler on the ascent, as if her patio sprint had vacuumed the air to follow her. Evie doesn't flick the light on as she enters her old room. The daylight presses through parted curtains, plenty enough for her old trophies and the neat geometry of the bedspread. She stands with her back to the door until her pulse slows.

Then she sits at the desk and reopens her laptop.

For a while, her only sounds are the faint whirr of the fan, the slow click of her own breath. On screen, the cursor blinks at her in pulse-matched rhythm. She doesn't need to check her notes to remember what's next; the moment in the backyard, that wind-stitched vision, has already cemented her resolve.

She opens the search window, types in "Southern Ohio + murder + lake + Janes." She adds "female victim," "unsolved," and the month her mother mentioned. The browser populates with a litany of small-town news sites, paywalled articles, a few PDF scans from local crime blogs. She clicks, scanning with a profiler's speed.

Within three links, she finds the headline: "Milford Woman Found Dead Near Perintown Woods." The photo is pixelated, amateur. The face is clear enough.

Evie stares. The world outside is muted, as if waiting.

The victim is named in the second paragraph: Emily Janes, 25, found by a power line worker who mistook her in the bushes for an injured deer. There is no mention of drugs, of known enemies. The write-up is padded with quotes from friends and relatives, none of which explain why Emily would end up dead in a heavily wooded area.

Evie copies the article into a new folder on her desktop. She labels it COLD CASE. The movement is reflexive, almost sterile, but the truth rattles her.

She opens another article. There's a school portrait: Emily as a senior, broad smile, those same streaks of blonde hair falling over one eye. She scrolls down, and the photo changes—Janes as a young adult, standing next to her older sister, hands folded just like Evie saw in the crosswalk.

It is the same woman. The blouse even looks familiar: white, button-down, a little loose at the shoulders. The collarbone visible, exactly as in the vision.

Evie shivers, but it isn't a chill from the room. It is the knowledge—the certainty—that whatever she saw wasn't a stress hallucination or garden-variety PTSD. She can picture in perfect detail the way Emily turned to look at her through the windshield, as if seeing her for the first time. The expression wasn't pleading, but neither was it indifferent. It was the stare of a problem hoping, against all odds, to be solved.

She lets the mouse hang over the photo for several seconds.

Out loud, softly, Evie says, "I saw you."

She doesn't expect an answer, and none comes.

Instead, Evie compiles the rest: police bulletin, reward poster, a brief forum thread where locals argue about whether the cops are doing enough. She dumps them all into the COLD CASE folder, then tags the contents with her own set of labels: wooded, power lines, barefoot, mother deceased. She adds one more: UNRESOLVED.

For a moment, she considers whether this is just another distraction. Whether the ghost is a metaphor or a curse. She thinks of all the cold cases she's ever worked—how the ones that stuck weren't the gory or sensational, but those that itched and needed scratching. The ones that wandered up at night, sat at the edge of your bed, and refused to let you sleep until you'd at least said their names.

Evie clicks back to the desktop, closes the tabs, and faces the wallpaper. She lays her palms flat on the table.

"I'll come back to you," she says, voice low, directed at the darkened screen. "Once I finish with Mercer."

She exhales and then opens the lid again.

Her next action is as practiced as any of her childhood routines. She launches the secure browser, enters her alias, and waits for the Tor network to connect. The delay is longer than she likes, but the clock says 4:07 PM, so traffic is up. Once inside, she navigates to their private group: not quite black market, not quite law enforcement, but the demilitarized zone where the two meet.

• Username: Black_Monday
• Password: [redacted]

She enters the forum. Her inbox shows one unread message, subject line: "Mercer Inquiry."

She opens it. The body is a single sentence:

> ROOTMUSE: Any update re: Zurich?

It's one of the core Ethos contacts. Likely the same person who fed her that first line about Mercer's health blackout.

> EVIE: Working this new angle. Need confirmation of Zurich event. Do you have location/date/time?

She hits send, but before the message disappears, a chat window pings. It's him, RootMuse again—at least she assumes he's a him.

> RootMuse: How did you get this channel?

> EVIE (Black_Monday): Questioning if I still have my badge?

> RootMuse: Not what I asked.

Evie waits, then types:

> EVIE: Guess you already know about my resignation. Still in system, at least for now. Need data on Mercer. Not having much luck.

The cursor blinks, then the reply:

> ROOTMUSE: Too bad. That'll be BAU's loss.

Evie stares. The chat is silent for four seconds, then:

> ROOTMUSE: Maybe yours too. Ethos has already confabbed on your next move. We're out. Not worth risk. Mercer has teeth.

Evie feels her jaw tighten. She considers the angle: Ethos helped her before, when it was just case files and background checks. Now, they sense something raw in her request—something worse. She hates that it's so obvious.

She tries a different approach.

> EVIE: There's a pattern in the Cartographer's homicides. Mercer is behind the scenes, not just observing. Any idea where he is right now?

> ROOTMUSE: Why the need to know?

> EVIE: He has answers, I intend to get.

> ROOTMUSE: His identity pings from many locations. Most are coming out of London. But, you know.

> EVIE: Yeah. I know. Just like I'm in Seattle.

There's a pause. Then, for the first time, RootMuse deviates from monosyllables.

> ROOTMUSE: This isn't a joke, Cross. Mercer's not the target you think. You go after him, it'll turn. You'll be next.

Evie stares at the monitor, fingers hovering. She thinks about what it would mean to let go of this, to accept defeat, to move back in with her parents and do nothing but cold-case spreadsheets until she's old and numb. The prospect is both comforting and revolting.

She types:

> EVIE: I'm already next. Don't care. But I want what you have on Zurich.

The reply comes instantly:

ROOTMUSE: Why do you think we'd help?

EVIE: Because you hate Mercer as much as I do.

ROOTMUSE: Not for free. Unemployed Mondays can't afford us.

Evie closes her eyes. She remembers the way the first Ethos chat went: back in Quantico, when she wore the badge and had the Bureau's muscle. Now, the power dynamic is reversed. She is the one reaching for scraps. The feeling is sickening.

EVIE: How much?

There's no answer.

She types again:

EVIE: I have evidence on your founder. The FBI never closed the case on the Chicago breach.

This time, the reply takes longer.

ROOTMUSE: Threats, Cross?

EVIE: Not a threat. Just data.

ROOTMUSE: Fine. You want a location? Zurich, Bahnhofstrasse, Hotel Felsenhof. Mercer checked in using a shell ID, left after two hours. Witness says he was with a woman, unknown. That's all.

Evie logs the address. She considers pushing for more, but knows the rhythm of the game: one trade at a time.

EVIE: Thanks.

ROOTMUSE: Don't mention it. Take that literally.

The window closes. The blue light of the screen fades, replaced by the sullen dark of her bedroom.

Evie stares at the desktop. The sense of isolation is total.

She glances again at the COLD CASE folder. At the face of Emily Janes.

The room is utterly quiet, except for the furnace click downstairs and the small, living sound of her own breath.

Evie leans back, hands behind her head, and tips her face to the ceiling. How much of her life has been spent waiting for people to talk, to confess, to answer? She has always been better with data than with living things. But now, the only data that matters is the kind no one wants to share.

After several minutes, she powers down the laptop. The room plunges from deep blue to gray, then to the kind of dark where every movement carries meaning.

Standing, she stretches, and goes to the window. There's no one there. Not even a ghost. Just the raw field, the rhododendrons, and the shadows cast by the porch light. She closes the curtain, sits on the bed, and lets the darkness seep. In her mind's eye, Emily Janes lingers. And behind her endless, starlit eyes, a shadow coils, calculating, waiting for a next move.

"No one's going to help me," she whispers. "I'm on my own."

Chapter Six

Connected Calls

She waits until the house is asleep—her father already snoring, her mother drifting off with the TV flickering from their bedroom—before opening the front door and stepping onto the porch. The November dark wraps the block tight; not a single window in the neighborhood is lit except the one she just left behind. There are no cars, not even in the far-off baseline of a passing truck. Just the wind and the shiver of old trees in the yard.

Her bottle of Knob Creek came from a local liquor mart—an impulse buy, or maybe a calculated one, depending on how much she wants to lie to herself. She sits on the porch swing, sets the bottle down, and tips two fingers' worth into a glass. The cold bites harder out here, and it's only after a long sip that her pulse stops fluttering.

The swing creaks under her slight sway.

For the first time since arriving, she lets her guard slip. The weight of the week—her parents' expectations, the endless data void around Mercer, supernatural crosswalks—presses down until she feels almost concave. Her breath fogs out into the night, every exhale dissipating in seconds.

She never liked being home. The silence here is not gentle; it is blunt, an anvil of expectation that crushes anything soft or unfinished. But tonight, she feels almost an armistice. She can just exist here, at least until morning.

The air wafts of distant rain and fading leaves. She tips the glass, draining her first go, and then just sits. There is no hurry. Nothing is going to change overnight.

Stray fireflies blink over the lawn, late survivors of a species that should have packed it in weeks ago. Their lights pulse at asynchronous intervals, a living Morse code she never learned. She pours again and tracks one as it zig-zags along the edge of the yard.

For a while, she tries to embrace the peace of this setting instead of dwelling. It's useless, of course—her brain always pulls the puzzle back in, like a tongue probing a cracked tooth. What is Mercer doing right now? What's his purpose? Is there even a point to any of this, or is she just the punchline to a cosmic joke, the only person in the Midwest who can't let go of a dead case and a dead child?

The bitterness surprises her. She thought she had burned through all of that years ago.

Evie leans back against the porch swing, closing her eyes and rotating the rosary on her wrist. She listens to the nothing. After a minute, she talks—not so much aloud, but inward to a space she can't quite see.

Harbinger.

She calls, not expecting a reply.

There's no manual for this. The entity or whatever it is does not always answer to prayer, nor respond to a summons or circles of salt. It appears to choose its own manner and expects her to surrender up to it. To 'give up the ghost' as they say, while leaving her somewhat wrecked but functional. She's attempted every form of logic and science to analyze it, all to no effect. Try as she might, it does not appear to be something that responds to control.

Still, tonight she needs something. A sign. A nudge. Even a hallucination would do, if it could point her to Mercer.

She breathes in slowly. Out slower.

"I don't know if you're in there," she whispers, "but if you are, I need a little help. Just a direction. A name. Something."

The gust sweeps by, but little else happens. Not even a tingle at the nape, not a shimmer at the edge of sight.

She tries again, this time shoehorning the memory of her daughter. Evie pictures June: the brown eyes, the lopsided smile, the chipped front tooth from falling off a bike. She holds it in her mind until the ache is physical. Then, she throws in Mercer's name like a dare.

If you're in there, show me.

Nothing.

She laughs, but it's a dry, twisted sound. "Didn't think so," she says, and refills the glass.

A car passes far off, and the noise echoes for a full minute before dying. Another firefly flicks in and out of existence over the porch steps. The world, as always, continues on as if she wasn't even there.

For a while, she just drinks and listens. Not for voices, not for anything supernatural. Just for herself. Her own breath, her own heart, and the slow way her body absorbs the cold while fueling warmth through whiskey.

It's at the bottle's dregs when she is given pause—not a touch, not a sound, but a narrowing of the world's focus, like a lens cranked tight. The night seems to slow. The last firefly hovers, almost static. Lawn shadows withdraw into themselves, sharp and intentional.

Evie sets the glass down. Her entire body vibrates. The hair on her arms stands, her pulse flicks in her ears, and a metallic taste fills her mouth.

At first, her vision grasps at a trick of the light—the shadows lengthening from the rhododendrons, the faint afterimage of fireflies. But then she's there, standing under their crabapple tree.

The blonde woman.

The one from the crosswalk, the backyard. Tonight, she is vivid, like a thing carved from moonlight and shadow. Her blouse is still white, but the bloodstain has grown, creeping down to the waist. The face is pale, eyes wide and so full of starlight that Evie almost recoils.

She squeezes her eyelids and checks again, but the apparition does not waver.

Evie stands, brushing grit from her palms, and forces herself down the steps, out onto the lawn. Her socks freeze instantly, but she ignores it.

"Okay," she says, voice low. "You have my attention."

The woman's mouth opens, but nothing emerges. Instead, her bloodstains pulse, and from the edges of the wound, motes of light leak out, rising and fading as they climb into the night. These are not random; Evie recognizes a pattern, though she can't place it. A cluster here, a streak there, each point blinking in and out of existence with an intelligence that feels cold and old.

Evie takes a step closer. The air between them shivers, and for a moment, it lights her inhalations with iron and ozone, as if a storm is about to break.

"What do you want?" she asks.

The ghost extends an open hand—not at Evie, but toward the driveway.

Evie turns, heart jack-hammering, and sees a man standing there. Not her father, not a neighbor. He is only a bit taller than herself, slender, wearing a T-shirt despite the weather. His face is soft around the chin, eyes dark and searching. He looks familiar, but Evie can't place him. She steps back.

"Who…" she begins.

The man says nothing. He lifts his shirt slowly, and reveals a hole in his torso—an absence, a wound. From the cavity, stars pour out, slow and deliberate, as if leaking from a cracked water cooler.

Evie's knees almost buckle.

She recognizes him then: the missing man from the Missouri news, the volleyball player, the one found dead in a park.

The man lowers his shirt, but the stars keep pressing out, pooling on the ground at his feet.

Evie staggers backward. "No, no, no," she mutters, hands clutching at nothing. This is not Mercer. This isn't what she asked for. She needs to—

The man raises a hand, pleading to her.

Evie feels the universe contract. There is no wind, no sound. She looks down and realizes her hands are empty. She left the whiskey glass on the porch.

She wheels to run, but a third figure blocks her path.

This one is new. It's a woman, early thirties with sun-kissed auburn hair. Her eyes are black, and her smile is crooked. She wears a red dress, an imprinted torn t-shirt, and the fabric around her belly is soaked through. As Evie watches, stars bubble up from her gut, swarm up her torso, and explode outward in a silent, glittering fountain.

The woman steps forward, closing the distance until they are nose to nose. Evie can't breathe.

Then, the woman leans in and whispers—not with words, but with the rush of wind through hollow places. Evie's brain flashes: three victims, three wounds, three sets of what? Each star that leaves the body is a lost piece.

She understands these are not random. They are cries.

A sharp pain blooms in her forehead. She drops to her knees. The world snaps back—the wind, the damp, the far-off hum of a neighbor's generator return to her reality. The others are gone now, but the afterimage of their wounds blazes behind her eyelids.

Evie drags herself to her feet. She staggers back onto the porch, fumbles for the whiskey glass, and finds it exactly where she left it.

Gripping the banister, she wills herself to stop shaking.

A drop of whiskey splashes onto the porch boards. It looks in the dim light exactly like another stain. She stares at it, and then at her trembling hands.

"Oh god," Evie whispers. "They're connected. They're all connected."

For the first time in days, she feels a sense of purpose. It's terrible, and clear, and undeniable. If there's a new killer out there—someone making wounds that spill the night—she will find them.

Maybe she's the only one who can.

Chapter Seven

Getting to Know

He rides through the city with the precision of the unimpressed. The pickup truck is a low-rent steed, but in this country, in this season, it blends as well as any car—nobody expects anything from a mud-stained F-150 except maybe a concealed weapon and a half-eaten McMuffin. Alexei navigates the swerve of the interstate with one knee, the other foot planted on the dash, and devotes his hands entirely to the phone. If the highway patrol is out tonight, let them try to explain to a judge how a man can swipe, drive, and compose entire dossiers without ever glancing at the road.

Downtown looms ahead, dazzling itself with holiday excess. The Liberty Memorial stands rigid in the distance, its vertical concrete shaft stabbing up through its floodlights. Tufts of flame erupt from its summit, washing the clouds in a prison-yard yellow. He has read that the monument is meant to honor the dead of old wars, but to him it's just an American obelisk—a totem to casualties.

He leaves the highway and dives into the arteries of the city proper. Union Station glows on his left, every column and clock face wrapped in desperate string-lights, windows packed with silhouettes of travelers queued up for nothing. There is a fullness to the air that reminds him, at least for a moment, of the festive crowds in Moscow's Red Square—though here, the volume is less. The streets pulse with a parade of battered sedans and white delivery vans.

At the red light, he lets the engine idle and focuses on his task.

There is efficiency in this country, but only for the ones who demand it. He scrolls through three different dating apps, none of which he finds especially intuitive, but all of which are serviceable enough. The user names amuse him. The faces, less so. He toggles between Bumble and Tinder with the studied boredom of a man who has already finished his work but needs to pretend otherwise.

His profile is a masterpiece of calculated appeal: "Alex, 31. World traveler. Biomedical engineering background, now in the Midwest for a consulting gig. Coffee, beer. Likes: museums, hiking, classical music. Dislikes: drama." The photos are recent, well-lit, and strategically cropped to suggest both humility and a hint of violence.

He knows what works.

The real algorithm, though, is not on the apps. It is in his head.

He has explained this to his previous buyer once. The mathematics of donor selection. Back in Russia, the state did it for you—conscription, orphanages, the unlucky in army hospitals. But here in America, you had to improvise. It's a market, and the best product wins. To maximize yield, you first cast a net of a hundred. Then, you vet for basic genetic potential. The Americans are thick with diabetes, obesity, and all the little failures of self-control. But not so much that you can't still find the gems—young, healthy, innocent enough to have lived clean.

After that, the rest is child's play.

He keeps a spreadsheet, of course. Each subject is assigned a color code and a subjective rating: likely, possible, substandard. The "duds" are eliminated at once: smokers, party girls, anyone with visible tattoos (potential for hepatitis), anyone mentioning chronic pain. Drug use is an automatic veto, though some recreational types he will consider—sometimes you need the organs, not the donor's resume. He narrows the list to a first set of ten, then rotates through them, messaging for dates. If he is lucky, five will respond.

He double-taps a girl's profile: dark hair, pale skin, eyes tilted just enough to suggest some Asian mixture. He cross-references her name on Facebook. She's a senior at UMKC, pre-med, volunteer for some animal shelter. Perfect. He likes them smart—it makes the last part more interesting.

A notification pops up: "You have a match!" He smiles and taps the conversation open.

Her first line: "So what brings you to KC?"

He types: "Long story. Will buy you a drink and explain everything. Are you free tonight?"

She responds in under thirty seconds: "Yes. Where?"

He glances at the time. It's already 8:14 PM. He prefers to do this early, but his schedule tonight is crowded. He has a second date. If the first is a bust, he can always pivot to the other.

He tells her, "There's a bar on the Plaza called O'Dowd's. Nine?"

"Sounds good," she says.

He logs the info in the spreadsheet, then returns to the main app. The second candidate is already messaging him, a grad student with an "old soul" and a taste for literature. He swipes left, not because she is unworthy, but because her profile mentions antidepressants in passing. He can't risk the interaction.

Lights change. He guns the engine and takes the curve onto Main, feeling the rear wheels slip for a fraction of a second before the traction reasserts. Plaza traffic is tighter, the air thick with the exhale of holiday cheer. The architecture is a kind of Spanish fantasy—terracotta roofs, white columns, iron filigree along the balconies. Every shop window is a diorama of winter longing: mannequins in faux fur, animated penguins, digital snowflakes projected onto the glass.

He finds street parking with shocking ease and idles a moment to compose himself.

Most men in this position would take a minute to check the hair, maybe pop a mint, dab the forehead with a napkin. Alexei has no use for such rituals. Instead, he recites his own checklist, internal and perfect.

Wallet: check. Phone charged. Teeth acceptable. Breath: vodka, but in this region nobody cares. Hands: steady, nails trimmed. He's worn his good coat—the subtle blue one, the fabric lightweight but warm. He adjusts the cuffs and kills the engine.

He sits for a moment longer, thinking of how the evening will proceed. First, the small talk. She will ask where he's from, about his work, about what it's like to have lived "so many lives." Alexei will answer with mild, self-deprecating stories, some of them even true. She will be nervous at first, but by the second drink her guard will slip. It always does.

Then he'll consider whether to sleep with her. The rule, self-imposed and thus sacred: never sex the ones you intend to harvest. Too much mess, too much risk. You can always take what you need later, if the opportunity returns. But if she doesn't qualify, if they prove less than worthy, he may just give her a night to remember. A mercy, really. Cold sex, instead of being added to his list.

He checks his phone, reads the match's profile again. Her name is Sam. She has a cat named Fibonacci. She ran a marathon two years ago. BMI estimated at 20.1, with visible muscle tone. She is exactly the type he was told to find.

His buyer—benefactor, as they prefer—never asks questions about the method. Only results. Alexei thinks, not for the first time, that this is the greatest flaw in American capitalism: nobody cares where the sausage is made, as long as it arrives on time. His shortcut is elegant, though. He suspects that if he ever explained it, his benefactor would be pleased. But for now, it is his own secret.

He glances up at the bar's neon sign, reflected in the windshield like a cartoon halo over his head.

"Поехали!," [Let's go!] he says, and grabs his phone and heads out.

The air is damp, as if a humidifier had been left on high. The crowd inside O'Dowd's is denser than he prefers, but not so tight that he can't spot her at once. She stands under the green awning, face upturned to the light, texting someone with furious two-thumb speed. As he closes the distance, she glances up, locks onto him with that practiced, app-taught eye-contact, and raises her hand.

She is smaller than the photos suggest. Most are. But her face is alive with nerves, her lips bitten raw, and he admires the effort she's put into the eyeliner. Her coat is secondhand but stylish. He notes her boots: flat heel, good for running, though he doubts she will.

"Alex?" she says, voice clipped by adrenaline.

He smiles, putting warmth into it. "Samantha, yes?"

She grins. "You can call me Sam. I'm glad you found the place."

He shrugs. "I find everything. It is my specialty."

She laughs, head tossing back just a little. The teeth are perfect. The gums: healthy, no signs of recession. He is already predicting her tissue type.

They walk inside together, crowd-pulsed, the air thick with beer and the scent of burnt bar food. The first drink is easy; she orders a cider, he takes vodka neat. They settle into a corner, where the din is manageable, and the table is just large enough to force proximity.

She asks, "So, tell me your story. Why Kansas City?"

He gives her the practiced version: postdoc at a research hospital, grants dried up, consulting for a medical device startup. He keeps the details vague, just enough for her to build a narrative in her head. People want stories. They don't care if they're true.

She asks about Bosnia. It's what he put on his profile. He laments the winters. Shares tidbits about wolves. She is fascinated, as they always are.

"Is it true Bosnians drink brandy with every meal?"

He smiles. "Depends. How strong the food versus the liquor."

She laughs, and so does he, though his mind is already doing the next round of analysis.

The girl does not drink too much. She is cautious, sipping slowly. Good. No liver issues. Her color is high, her hands steady, eyes never break from his for more than three seconds at a time. She is competitive, likely driven by some invisible ghost of a father. He marks her at 95% of the template.

The conversation drifts. She asks about music. He quotes some classical composers, throws in a joke about Shostakovich, and is rewarded with a real laugh.

She says, "You're not like the other guys on these apps."

He leans in, just to remind her that distance is optional.

"And what are the other guys like?" he asks.

She rolls her eyes. "You know. Boring. Horny. Aggressively dull. Half of them never make it through the actual date."

He raises his glass. "To the exceptional," he says.

She clinks her cider against it. "To the exceptional."

He finds, to his surprise, that he is enjoying this. She is quick, sharper than the first impression. There is a layer of sadness under her jokes, a thing he recognizes and, in a strange way, respects.

Alexei watches her as she finishes her cider. She is searching unconsciously for a cue from him—whether the night is over, whether to take this somewhere else, whether she should already be preparing her escape. He decides.

"Walk with me?" he says, voice soft.

She smiles. "I'd like that."

They leave the bar, the holiday lights brighter now, the air thickening with the promise of snow. He takes her arm, not because he needs to, but because it feels right. She is warm, the pulse in her wrist rapid and hard.

They walk along the river, under strings of colored bulbs, past herds of other couples doing the same dance. He listens to her talk about school, about her thesis, about the dog she wants when she finally escapes this city. She never asks him what he wants. Nobody ever does.

At the bridge, she pauses. Looks up at him. The wind tangles her hair.

"Do you want to come up to my place?" She asks, and for a moment he sees a flicker of doubt behind the bravado.

He runs a scenario tree: up to the girl's place; she offers him something—coffee, a shot, maybe a story about a dead pet or an ex-boyfriend who still lurks on the block. He could take her up and end the night the way most do—messy, half-remembered.

But that is not the purpose. Not tonight. She is an ideal candidate, maybe better than what he promised on the list. To sleep with her would be to risk contamination, or worse, loss of access. He needs her unmarked, unwary, still propelled by whatever ache makes her walk with men like him. He needs to leave this for next time.

He grins, lets a hint of shyness cross his face, as if she's caught him off guard.

"Nah," he says. "Tonight I prove I am gentleman." He makes a show of hands raised for surrender. "Let's not go too quick."

It is the correct move. Sam shoulders into him, bumping him back. "Oh, playing hard to get then. All right. I see how it is." She gives him a coy look. "Another night then?"

"I would like that. Yes. How you say—rain check?" he counters.

Her gaze lingers on Alexei a bit before she turns and departs. The city is even colder now. The lights dim as he casually stalks back to where he parked.

Alexei sits in the truck, hands on the wheel, and for a moment allows himself to feel the ache of fatigue. He marks her as a good candidate, not a certainty. The scar is a minor trait, but the rest of her is perfect.

He starts the engine, pulls away from the curb, and melts into the city's sleeping dark. There is still a second date to be made. Still more games to play.

Alexei wonders idly if this is what Americans call "the pursuit of happiness." He doubts it. But he's never been one to question the logic of the hunt.

Chapter Eight

Can't Stop

Evie wakes at 6:11, though her body tells her it's closer to four. For a while, she lies flat on her back, arms at her sides, and listens to the old house recalibrate around her. The air vent ticks with intermittent heat; the far-off shift of the water heater. There is, outside her childhood window, only the faint blue of predawn.

Giving herself the extra minute, she swing-sits up, feet to floor, and Evie's day begins.

She dresses in sequence: thermal, blouse, jeans, then her gray winter jacket. Her bag is already half-packed, the contents methodical and spare. She stashes the laptop first, then the envelope of case files—each printout hand-labeled with the victim's name and date, a procedural anchor against the feeling that she is chasing literal phantoms. Next, her phone, charger, and a pillbox with exactly five Adderall and two long-expired sleep aids, which she keeps as a talisman rather than a solution.

The last item is the Mercer dossier. She runs a thumb along its edge. Part of her wants to tear it up, salt the earth, never let the name into her mind again. The rest of her is not so delusional. *Not without answers.*

She places it at the bottom of the bag, beneath everything else, and zips the main compartment closed.

Opening the door quietly, she treads softly down the stairs, muscle memory keeping to the parts that don't squeak. There is no movement in the living room, but the kitchen emits a soft, slow-motion hum—the refrigerator, plus an intermittent tapping.

She rounds the corner and sees her mother, already awake. Carol Whitaker sits in a bathrobe, fingernails maintaining a steady cadence on the table. A mug steams in her left hand. For a second, Evie considers reversing back up the stairs and trying again in an hour.

But her mother has already turned. "You're up early," she says. "I thought you'd sleep in."

Evie enters, careful with the threshold. "I don't sleep much," she says, both as a fact and a plea for no follow-up.

Mom studies her for a moment—real scrutiny, not the friendly kind. "And you're packed."

"Yeah." Evie nods. "I need to get going. There's that thing in Missouri."

She expects a protest, or at least a sigh, but her mother only stares. "You just got here."

Evie shrugs. "Doesn't mean I stop being me."

Her mother's lips press together. "Coffee?"

"Yes, please."

The next minute is choreographed. Her mom moves with brisk, efficient steps, pouring from the machine, adding creamer. She slides the mug across the counter, exactly as she's done a hundred times before. Evie takes it, sips.

Leaning back against the sink, Mom's arms fold. "You going to tell me what's so important?"

"Hard to say." Evie looks at her hands. "It's work."

Carol's eyebrows tilt. "Last I heard, you don't work for them any-more."

A pause. "Doesn't mean I can't help."

A moment lingers, where neither wants to fill with words. The only sound is the fridge's condenser, cycling through its tiny cold war.

The kitchen clock shows 6:29 when Dad enters, clad in sweatpants and a T-shirt that reads "DAVIDSON'S FEED & TACK." He surveys the scene, sees the bag by the door, and grunts. "Morning, girls."

Mom pours another mug, black. She hands it to him, and in the transfer, squeezes his hand. He reads her mood instantly.

He sits at the table facing Evie. "You heading out now?" His tone is all business, the strategy of not making a big deal out of anything that's already decided.

She nods. "The earlier, the better. I want to hit Missouri by noon."

He sips, then: "Your oil changed?"

"Last week."

"Windshield wipers working?"

"Yes, Dad."

He grins, soft at the edges. "Can't help it. You know I have to ask."

She lets herself smile. "I know."

Mom retrieves a travel thermos from the drying rack and begins to pour. "You eating before you go?"

Evie shakes her head. "Not hungry."

Henry raises his mug in a half-toast. "You're usually hungry."

"Not as much lately."

A silence, longer this time.

Her mother steps in. "What's this really about, Evie?"

Evie thinks of the faces from the porch the night before—the blonde woman, the man with the gut void, the auburn-haired vision whose wound spurted stars instead of blood. She thinks of the pattern, the sense of compulsion, the fact that none of her explanations would survive the morning daybreak.

Instead, she settles on, "It just feels like the right thing to do."

Carol leans closer. "You look tired."

Evie can only shrug. "Everyone's tired."

Mom frowns. "You know, sometimes you get a look. I don't think you realize."

Evie does not answer. Instead, she opts to add the rest of her coffee into the travel thermos and twists the lid shut.

"I wish you'd let us help you," Mom says, voice nearly breaking. "Just tell us what you're really running from."

Evie closes the zipper on her bag. "It's not like that. I'm not running."

Carol's eyes shine in the gray kitchen light. She reaches out and touches Evie's wrist, her hand cool from the counter. "You never really came home, did you?" It isn't a question, not really.

Evie holds the touch for a second, then withdraws. "What I'm searching for isn't going to be found here," she says. Then, seeing her mother's face, she softens it: "I mean—I can't stay. Not right now."

Her father stands, finishes his coffee in a single pull. "Just promise you'll text when you get there."

"I will," Evie says.

He wraps her in a brief, tight hug, the sort of hug men use when they're trying not to communicate anything but necessity. Then he steps aside, lets her mother in. Carol hugs longer, hands gripping the fabric of Evie's jacket.

"Be careful," she whispers.

Evie says nothing. She picks up her bag, slings it over her shoulder, and heads for the door.

Outside, the first chill of morning lies heavy on the grass, silvering the yard and crisping the breath as she exhales. She opens the trunk, drops the bag in, and stands with the lid open for a half-beat, letting the cold into her skin.

She glances back at the house. In the kitchen window, both parents stand framed, side by side, each holding their mugs. They look smaller in this context, reduced by distance and glass, but also more connected. She gives them a nod, then closes the trunk.

The drive would be only seven hours to get there if she drove straight through. But there will be a stop in Milford along the way. Who knows how long that detour may take. Yet, it is no less important. There are reasons for her visions. Best to start at the beginning.

She unlocks the car, slides in, and warms the engine. The radio is off, phone already synced and waiting. She backs down the drive in reverse, then shifts into drive and pulls away.

In the mirror, the house shrinks, the front porch lamp pales against the blue-black dawn. The sight burns itself in as a kind of afterimage—family, stilled and suspended, the echo of home retreating mile by mile.

She does not look back again.

Chapter Nine

Kept

The Milford Mortuary sits on a corner lot between a Catholic cemetery and an insurance office with a faded "Honk If You Love Jesus" magnet on the door. The building itself is one story, ranch-style, the kind of postwar architecture that aspires to look less like a place for the dead and more like a well-maintained dentist's office. Evie parks at the end of a row, away from the other cars. She exits, locks the door behind her, and inhales the cut-cedar chill of morning.

Inside, the air holds competing scents: lemon and last week's carnations. The lobby is a sequence of beige, from the walls to the couch to the low-pile carpet that flexes under her boots. Hallmark efforts are maintained to keep things presentable: the corners bear silk flower arrangements in bronze urns, and a flat-screen TV over the check-in desk cycles through a slideshow of sunset beaches and calligraphy verses about remembering.

Reception is empty. There is a bell on the counter, but Evie skips it. She scans the room. On a side table sits a black binder, open to a page with pics of the recently venerated—photo, name, dates. She flips until she finds Janes, Emily R., then closes the book.

A door at the far end opens, and the mortician steps out. He is younger than she expected, maybe early fifties, with hair cropped close and his tie cloud white. His eyes seem fatigued for this late in the morning. He clocks Evie at once, reads her stance, and approaches.

"Can I help you?" he asks.

Evie begins to reach for a badge, then just says, "I'm following up on Emily Janes. I understand you handled the... arrangements."

He doesn't nod, just tilts his head. "Yes, I did. Are you with the family?"

"No," she replies. "Just trying to close the loop. Recovering ground, in case anything was overlooked in the initial investigation."

There is a flicker of something, then the mortician's hands find their way into the pockets of his coat. "Most inquiries are through the police or next of kin."

Evie nods. "I'm not with the local PD. Consider me more like a consultant. I'm interested in the condition of the remains. Details not covered in the public reports."

He hesitates as the room subtly shifts: a bit cooler, not by degrees but by sensation, as if a door somewhere has been left open. Grayson—she sees his name on the tag now—seems to feel it too. His eyes flit to the thermostat, then back to her.

The man surveys her. "I have some time before my next viewing. If you'd like to discuss, my office is back here."

"That would be great," Evie says.

He leads her down a hallway tiled with off-white squares. The walls are lined with what might charitably be called 'art'—oil landscapes of the Ohio River, prints of lighthouses standing against scenic storms. Grayson opens the third door on the left. The office is small, windowless, and dominated by a desk and filing cabinets.

He gestures to a chair. Careful to keep her posture open, she takes it. No crossed arms, no legs angled away. Her entire bearing is, if anything, slightly receptive, as though she's the one here for an interview.

Grayson sits, folding his hands over a legal pad. "This is irregular," he says, but not in protest.

Evie exuded openness, receptive to any tells: the way his fingers twitched when he said 'irregular,' the slight flare of his nostrils at each exhale. She's familiar with this performance. He's trained himself to appear imperturbable, but grief, violence, and bureaucratic audits have probably cracked him a hundred times before.

She leans in. "Emily Janes. Given your experience, is there anything about her that stands out?"

He shrugs. "She was brought in under her family's wishes, after the autopsy. Coroner shared some routine tests—blood loss, exposure. Nothing hazardous."

Evie considers the protocol. "No sign of drugs?"

"None. Clean bloodwork, which is unusual these days."

A pause. She lets it hang. "Cause of death?"

"Officially? Shock and exsanguination." He looks at his hands. "But it was really the wounds."

She raises her brow a fraction. "Go on."

He uncrosses, recrosses his ankles. "They were surgical, not medical; precise, layered. She was opened before the autopsy. Almost as if the monster that did it had medical training. Amateur but practiced."

Evie continued, "Anything about the body they didn't put in the file? Was there a necklace? A ring? Any jewelry?"

He stares at the ceiling as if replaying a scene. "No. Any clothing would be kept as evidence, but I understand most of it was gone by the time they found her."

Evie writes nothing down. She memorizes every word.

"Was there anything about the wounds themselves—anything not strictly in the report?" she asks. "Sometimes things get left out."

He hesitates, then says, "I've handled a lot of ODs, suicides, the standard trade. But this—Emily was just gone. Hollowed out."

Evie lets that word settle. "Hollowed?"

"Not at first glance. Everything looked in place, but when I got in there—it was almost like someone had taken a tour, touched every organ, and then left." He shudders, just a fractional movement, but Evie catches it. "Corneas were gone. So were the kidneys, and the liver. Then someone stitched her up."

"Not a typical death," she observes.

He shakes his head. "No. There were no ragged edges, no mess. Whoever did it was clean, almost... reverent."

His body gave off cues: the gooseflesh rising on his forearms, the way his pupils narrowed. But apparently, he was not the only one paying attention—a low, sifting sadness permeated from within herself.

Evie holds his gaze. "Did you take this case personally?"

Cupping his hands over his mouth, Grayson closed his eyes. "I knew her."

Evie's head tilts. "How?"

"Not well," he says, voice tight. "She used to bring flowers to her grandmother's grave. Every Sunday, rain or shine. I'd see her through the window, talking to the headstone. Sometimes she'd wave." His smile is a mangled thing. "She often came alone."

The air in the office dips another degree. Not cold like winter, but like the deep cellars where old grief is stored. Evie's chest pulses—she can almost feel the sadness leeching through her, into every part of her that isn't pure calculation.

"She didn't deserve this," Grayson says.

"No one does," Evie replies. The words are a reflex, but something softens at the end. She is not accustomed to comfort, either giving or receiving it.

He sits for a long moment, hands in his lap. Then, almost as an afterthought, he reaches for the bottom drawer of a file cabinet. It sticks, then gives. Grayson removes a small, white envelope, the kind used for cash tips.

The man slides it across the desk. "I probably shouldn't be giving you this. Against protocol. But I kept it."

Evie picks up the envelope. It weighs almost nothing. She glances at him for permission, then opens it.

Inside is a zip-bagged single lock of blonde hair.

"I clipped it before she was cremated," Grayson says. "I don't know why. Call me crazy. I just... felt like someone might need it someday."

Evie folds the envelope closed, places it in the inner pocket of her coat. She meets Grayson's eyes for the first time, and lets a small, real gratitude slip through. "Thank you," she says, and means it.

He nods, and in the silence that follows, she senses the weight lifting from him—a fraction, but measurable.

She stands. "I'll give you my cell number. If you remember anything else, feel free to reach out."

He nods again. "You seem like the kind of person who remembers what's important."

She offers a hint of a smile. "I try."

Her exit is quick. She leaves Grayson in his office. The lobby is still deserted; the scent of lemon is now sharp enough to cut through the floral overtones.

Out in the sunlight, Evie pauses, envelope secure, and draws a long breath. That lock of hair seems to press through the fabric, light as a secret. It will matter, in some way she cannot yet predict.

For a moment, she watches the traffic on the street—morning still thick with the slow-motion of people who have somewhere to go. Climbing into her car, she inserts the envelope into her bag, and buckles in. The presence within her remains calm, the sadness subsides to a dull ache. Her next step is clear. She will follow the pattern wherever it leads.

The ignition turns, engine humming. She glances once more at the mortuary, then at the blue sky, which is not so much cheerful as impartial. For now, that is enough.

Chapter Ten

Available Insights

The Lincoln County Sheriff's Office is a flat-roofed brick after-thought wedged between a Veterinarian and two modest strip malls. There's a sandwich board by the curb promising 'Handgun Safety Class: All Welcome,' but the parking lot is empty except for two patrol cars and a minivan with body damage on both sides. Evie's Ford Fiesta has no difficulty in selecting a parking space.

The foyer's heat is cranked to press back the cold, blowing at her as she passes into the lobby. A reception window manned by a dispatcher clocks her at once—mid-thirties, slight, alone—and puts on a greeting smile that fails to reach his eyes.

"Ma'am?" He says it with a patient twang.

"Evelyn Cross, here to see Sheriff McAllister," Evie says. Not un-intentionally, her FBI lanyard just peeks out from under her coat. Technically, it's not valid, her badge privileges on administrative ice, but the hint still has its magic.

The dispatcher's eyes flick to the card, then back to her face. A ten-count passes, then, "He's in. I'll text him and bring ya through."

Doors here are the hollow-core sort, the kind that sound a ricochet of footsteps ahead of you. She follows the man down the hall, past a cluster of cubicles where two deputies are hunched over a monitor, elbows nearly touching. There is the faint, sweet smell of banana bread, probably from the break room, and a hint of shoe polish. The walls bear fading photos of Boy Scout troops and little league plaques that ended five years back.

The Sheriff's office is at the far end, labeled simply: SHERIFF. Inside, McAllister stands with his back to the outside window, thumb-scrolling on his phone, the other hand planted on the desk like he's bracing for recoil. He looks up.

"Agent Cross," he says, voice equal parts cordial and sandpaper. "Wasn't expecting anyone from the Bureau."

Evie accepts the handshake. It is firm, dry; the kind learned from years of fairgrounds and getting voted into office.

"Thanks for making time, Sheriff. I'm only in town a day or two, just caught the news story while I was passing through."

He cocks his head, sets the phone down, and offers her a seat. His desk is organized in the way of someone who expects a surprise inspection: all files edge-aligned, a mug of pens like bayonets at the ready. — Respect.

"Let me guess. You're one of them profilers, am I right?" McAllister asks, crossing to his own chair.

"Good call. Guess that's why you're the Sheriff," Evie says. "No need for concern, though. I wasn't sent here. Technically, I'm on leave. I figured since I was headed this way I'd offer any help. More of a courtesy, not a federal intrusion."

She says it with the softness of an olive branch, and he picks it up. The tension in his shoulders drops a half-inch. "This office runs a lot on guesswork and caffeine. The more eyes, the better." Then, as if embarrassed by the sentiment, he pivots: "You want coffee? Got a fresh pot. Missouri's best, or so we're told."

She hesitates just enough to keep the exchange equal. "Maybe later."

McAllister looks her over again, recalibrates his approach. "So, the Cuivre River Park case then?"

She drops the preamble: "That's the one. I understand he was last seen at a sports bar? I'd like a walk-through of the last twenty-four. If you can share anything off-book, I may be able to offer some insights."

He nods, face going grave. "Awful thing. Lawrence Holloway—I knew the boy's mother. Used to bowl with her back when there was a league." He reaches into a drawer and brings out a thin folder, slides it across. "But to be honest, I think *we're* up to the challenge."

Evie catches on the "we're." She opens the folder, but before digesting the page, the Sheriff's eyes flick over her shoulder.

"Detective Hayes," he says. "You got a sec?"

Evie turns. The man is broad-shouldered, not tall but built like a brick wall set on edge. His hair is cropped tight and going steel-gray at the temples, skin deeply etched with sun. He wears jeans with a pressed crease, an MSHP badge clipped to his belt, and the cautious posture of a man who's seen more than his share of crime scenes. A handshake is not offered; instead, he gives her a nod that says, 'I see you.'

Hayes's tone is low, eased. "You the profiler?"

She nods. "Evelyn Cross. Just Evie, if you like."

He grunts in response. "Make it out of Quantico much?"

She offers a neutral smile. "Once or twice."

McAllister gestures to the small table in the corner. "Why don't you both have a seat? We can hash it out better here than in the hallway."

Hayes sits. He laces his hands on the tabletop and fixes Evie with a look that is not challenge but scrutiny, the way a bloodhound sizes up another canine—no threat, but no deference, either.

"Have an interest, then?" he says.

"Also, would like a sense of the local context," Evie replies. "What wasn't written down?"

Hayes leans back. "Small town, everybody knows everybody. That's the context."

"Except," McAllister cuts in, "when they don't. This one's riding atop the more conspiratorial neighbors. Black vans, strangers, the works." He gives Hayes a sideways glance, and it's clear they've had this debate before.

Evie flips through the folder. "I'm interested in the medical side. Autopsy's not fully in the system, but the preliminary says exsanguination."

Hayes cocks his head, eyes not leaving hers. "They left him clean. Not much blood, no mess. Coroner says it was like he went in for an oil change and they forgot to refill him."

"Any witnesses?"

The Sheriff and Hayes both shake their heads in unison.

"Not unless you count a homeless guy who swears it was aliens," McAllister says.

"Oh, I don't know." Evie smirks. "I've learned not to overlook the down-and-out."

Hayes's gaze softens, just enough to mark the transition from suspicion to curiosity. "You see a lot of this back east?"

"Used to," Evie says, "...before cross-state algorithms. These days, convictions are up, and we're hammering those numbers down." The admission is more candid than she intended, but the man's expression reads: Respect.

She closes the folder and sets it back down. "How about the coroner?"

Hayes nods. "That's Dr. Kim. She's off duty till three. You want to wait... or?"

Evie senses the invitation. "I could use a bite. Any place around here not a grease trap?"

Hayes's lips twitch. "You like pie?"

Evie grins. "Always."

"There's a diner across the road. Coffee's bad, but the pie is a redeemer. Plus, it's the only option within walking distance."

McAllister waves a hand. "Take your time. I'll be here."

As the two rise, the Sheriff gives Evie a look she reads as both gratitude and relief. For all the local pride, there's a comfort in sharing a piece of the nightmare with someone else.

Hayes opens the door for her, letting her walk ahead. Outside, the cold is razor-thin. The diner sign flickers across the street: Lucky's Lunch, all red neon and blacked-out bulbs. Hayes keeps his hands in his pockets, head angled down like a man waiting out a storm.

Evie can't help herself. "You ever get the sense that some cases are just... handed down?"

He looks up, meeting her eyes. "Every damn time."

They cross together, boots crunching on salt. For the first time in months, Evie feels a ghost of belonging—maybe not family, but hauntingly somewhere around there. Again, he holds the door for her, and the noise and sugar swallow the two into the heat of the place.

Chapter Eleven

Lessons in Oversharing

The interior of Lucky's is a time capsule, like someone locked it in amber in 1985 and forgot to stop the clocks. Booths are vinyl, cracked and re-taped in places, the stuffing yellowed like old teeth. A counter runs the length of the front, with red-topped stools that list slightly to port. Walls are smeared with sun-faded posters for pie, Coca-Cola, and the annual county fair. There is a smell—bacon, fryer oil, and a faint cleanser from whatever was used to wipe down the tables at the start of the shift. The only music is from a tabletop jukebox on each booth, most not plugged in but all of them filled with the memories of songs past.

Evie and Hayes choose a booth near the back, the one under a faded pennant for the St. Louis Cardinals. He waits for her to sit first, then slides in opposite, elbows planted wide, hands flat on the table. She notes the posture, the calm assumption of physical space—classic local cop, but softened by his neutral blue eyes and the way he keeps his voice at half-volume.

A waitress comes over, bringing water without being asked. She glances at Evie, recognizes her as not-from-here, and gives a perfunctory smile. "Coffee?" she offers.

"Two," Hayes says. "Black for me."

"Cream and one sugar," Evie adds.

The waitress disappears, and Hayes takes a second to inventory the morning regulars: a pair of ancient farmers in seed caps, a young couple with a toddler, and a man in scrubs reading the sports section. Evie matches the rhythm, eyes scanning, cataloging the power structure of the room in a single sweep.

Hayes leans in, voice pitched so no one else can hear. "So. You from Haden's shop, or are you soloing this?"

"Haden?" Evie blinks, then recovers. "Not exactly. I worked under him at Quantico. These days, I've switched back to being more a freelance analyst." She lets it hang, to see if he'll ask about the hiatus. He doesn't.

"I heard of Haden's crew. Never saw one up close." He gives her a half-smile. "Expected they'd be more... tall."

Evie shrugs. "I was the budget option."

That gets a proper smile from him, quick but genuine. "You work many like this?"

She shrugs again. "Not in a while. For the last couple of years, my focus was mainly on financial crimes. Most of the time it was spreadsheets, not bodies." She doesn't mention why she switched, or why she left. He seems to understand.

The waitress returns, mugs in hand. She pours, leaves the pot, along with a few packets and a bell creamer, then vanishes without a word. Hayes takes a sip, grimaces.

"Never changes," he says. "You can taste every moment it sat on the burner."

Evie tries hers. He's not wrong.

A pause, the comfort of two professionals calibrating their meters.

She makes the opening gambit. "The body—cleaned out, no blood, anything I'm missing?" She watches his face for the micro-twitches.

He doesn't. "Coroner is off the record, but yeah. Exsanguination was secondary; then there was the harvest. She says she's seen only one other like it, and that was in Chicago, years ago."

Evie nods. "I gather you tried digging into the dark web. Am I right?"

He looks up, with a flicker of interest. "You know the playbook. My guys ran it, spent the last few days trying to sniff out anyone soliciting, any weird sales. Came up dry."

"That's expected." She gives him a small, almost pitying smile. "Most of the listings you find online are scams or stings. The real sales happen off-platform, invite-only. A closed loop, with maybe a few trusted brokers in between. By the time you see a hint, the thing's already being implanted halfway across the country."

He drums his fingers on the table, liking the sound of her logic. "You ever see one go sideways?"

"In theory. But it's rare. The buyers are more careful than the sellers. Most of the time, the organs don't even stay domestic. Higher value in the Gulf States or Singapore."

He lets out a breath, slow and even. "Hell of a world, isn't it?"

She doesn't answer, not directly. Instead, she leans back and gives him a look that says she's not here to judge.

"So what's your next move?" he asks. "I can tell you the sheriff wouldn't mind a profile. Not something we'd feed to the press, more like where to look next."

Evie considers her words. "Could be a local, or at least someone comfortable enough to stage a body that way and not get seen. But the actual removal? Not exactly amateur, but not hospital grade either. I'm guessing portable equipment, not a lab." She hesitates, recalling her browse over the Sheriff's file. "The victim profile is somewhat unusual, being male—but no health problems, no lifestyle risk factors. These traits make for a quality selection, so not likely random."

"Random is rarely random, not in these cases," he says.

"True. There's always a reason." Evie pauses. She hasn't mentioned the Janes case. That would certainly interest—Something clamps inside her, a fist around her lungs. It squeezes, constricts.

Hayes doesn't notice. He's already thinking ahead. "You think he'll do it again?"

She wants to say yes. Evie wants to say that he already has, that there's a blonde girl in Milford whose wounds probably match this one. But as she opens her mouth, a chill seizes her ribcage, stops her breath in transit.

She blinks once, hard. The diner seems to flicker, just for a second. The air grows sharper, electric. A headache starts behind her eyes, rapid onset. And a vague sense permeates her core—No.

Hayes' brow furrows. "You all right?"

She forces a smile. "Fine. Just—blood sugar drop."

He slides the pie menu across the table. "They have the cure for that here. Lemon is their signature best."

She shakes her head, but the gesture feels stiff. The pressure in her chest swells. The urge to say something about Emily Janes, about the past Cartographer case—it burns in her throat, a reflux of truth.

She tries anyway. "There was another. In Ohio. Girl named Emil—"

The pressure spikes, white-hot. For a second, her vision blurs.

And then, their tabletop jukebox—dead since the first Bush administration—jerks to life. It clicks, whirring and flipping, the selector arm skipping through a dozen songs at blinding speed. The noise is sharp, violent, out of place. Every head in the diner turns, the waitress drops a spoon, the toddler at the window wails.

Hayes jumps, nearly upending his coffee. He looks under the table, searching for a cause. "What the hell—"

The jukebox's plastic face flashes, then the sound cuts out as abruptly as it started. The room falls into a tense silence, every eye fixed on their booth.

Hayes, embarrassed, reaches under and yanks the plug. "Sorry. Didn't mean to—" He tries to laugh it off, but his laughter has an edge.

Meanwhile, Evie barely breathes. The pressure in her chest eases, replaced by a ringing in her ears. She knows on some level that this is not just an electrical malfunction. The Harbinger has spoken in its own language. Don't. Not yet.

Hayes is the first to recover. He looks at her with genuine concern now. "You sure you're okay? You went pale."

She nods, breathing through it. "Just got lightheaded. It's nothing."

It's obvious he doesn't buy it, but still allows her to slide. The rest of the diner gradually returns to its business. The toddler, appeased with a jelly packet, resumes finger-painting the window. Their waitress watches from behind the counter, eyes narrowed.

Evie stands abruptly, desperate for cold air. "I should get going. Thank you for the coffee."

He stands as well, blocking her exit for just a second. "You don't have to run."

"I do," she says, and means it.

He reaches into his wallet and slides his card across the table. "All right. I tell you what, if you think of anything... want to share something helpful, or just a sounding board, you can reach me here."

She takes it, but doesn't meet his eye.

Stepping aside, Liam opens the way. "Seriously. If nothing else, I've grown into being a good listener."

She hesitates at the threshold, then looks back at him. His expression is equal parts worry and something else—respect, maybe, or a shade of an earlier, less-cynical self.

"Thank you," Evie says.

He feigns tipping his hat to her. "Be safe, Agent Cross."

She walks out; the bell on the diner door jangles in the gust.

Outside, the air is a bracing slap. She stands on the sidewalk and breathes until her heart slows. The card in her palm is warm.

She wants to believe she could have stayed, talked about anything, maybe even had a slice of pie and pretended the world wasn't full of bodies and spirits and wounds that never close. But she knows nothing holds her for long. Not people, not places, not even her own skin.

Still, as she stands outside her car, Evie pulls out her phone, thumbs open a message, and types:

> EVIE: Thanks again for the bad coffee, and the company. I'll let you know if anything shakes loose.

She hesitates, then adds:

> EVIE: Next time, I'm picking the song.

Evie hits send, slides the phone into her pocket. She looks across the street, to the window and Liam's slight grin at reading her text. She lets herself smile, just for a second.

Then Evie climbs in, starts the engine, and drives away.

Chapter Twelve

That One

E vie pulls into a parking lot, drawn in by the 'Quiet Comfort Motor Lodge' signage, on the outskirts of Moscow Mills. She parks, kills the engine, and sits with both hands on the wheel until the heater's blow turns cold.

Check-in is, blessedly, contactless. A man behind plexiglass slides her keycard through a drawer, says, "Evening, ma'am," then returns to his marathon of YouTube videos. Her room is on the second floor, end of the row. It promises a river view, but the actual vista is an unlit drainage canal and the broken-down hulk of a playground merry-go-round.

Inside, the room is everything she expects: two queen beds, both made with hospital-cornered polyester; a functional but war-worn desk; and, above the TV, a still-life of mallards flaring for a landing on a fictional lake. She clicks the deadbolt, draws the curtain, and lines her boots beside the heater.

Evie drops her overnight on the nearest bed and paces twice, letting herself acclimate. Even with her phone on silent, the phantom buzz of the outside world hums along her nerves. She ignores it for now.

First things first: recon on herself. She tugs off her jacket, catches her reflection in the TV's black screen, and stares.

Her own face startles her. The exhaustion, sure. But also a rawness in the eyes that wasn't there before—something that looks out-of-place even on her own features. She sits on the edge of the bed and opens her laptop, not ready to face the mirror yet, but unable to stop herself from replaying the missed pie with Hayes.

The Harbinger. The way it surged in her chest at the mere mention of the Janes case. Its force, the way the world tunneled down to a pinpoint of pressure. And then the diner, its jukebox animated by a will not her own, the message was clear: Don't.

She has questions. She always does. But she also knows, for whatever is inside of her, that direct address is rarely rewarded—if anything, maybe it damn well amuses the thing.

Fine, she'll try anyway.

Evie stands, flips on the bathroom light, and faces herself in the mirror. The fluorescent hum makes the glass vibrate with a low-grade hostility.

"All right," she says, voice steady. "You got my attention. I hope you're pleased with yourself. But if you think for one second, I'm going to let you run this show—"

The words die, swallowed by the faintest movement at the edge of the glass. She could swear for half a heartbeat that the shadow in the bathroom corner shifted. She holds her ground.

"You can cut the cheap tricks," she says, softer now. "We want the same thing, don't we? To stop some bastard? To get some kind of closure, even if it's not for me?"

Evie waits. Nothing.

She tries to summon her best profiler's cool, but it's hard to play chess with an opponent who lives on her every nerve. She lets out a tight, dry laugh. "That's what I thought," she says, and flicks the light off.

Glad we had this talk.

Back at the desk, she flips open her laptop and sets up shop. Two browser windows: one for the Bureau's dwindling-access feed, still trickling files to her old email in-basket, and one for the open internet, filtered for patterns the FBI usually miss. She burns through articles on organ trafficking, trying to pin down a motive—something she can offer as a profile before another body turns up.

Most of the write-ups are years old copy-and-paste, rehashing the familiar tropes: "black market," "Eastern European syndicates," "the price of a human heart on the global market." Nothing new. She cross-references the last year of disappearances, focusing on what isn't said in the news reports. This is her superpower, really—not seeing what's present, but triangulating the holes.

After forty minutes, a news article from ten months ago catches her eye: "Texas Woman Survives Ordeal After Kidney Theft." Clickbait title. She nearly skips it, but the timestamp is right: the same week as a spike in organ-donor euphemisms comes from to dark web. The piece is shallow, but the subject of the article is not. Laney Jo Rayburn, 27, survived a 'targeted abduction' in which she awoke in a hotel bathtub, minus one kidney, and called her own ambulance.

The accompanying photo is surprising. Laney is standing in front of the hospital, a honey-blonde broad, dressed in a cheap denim jacket, thrusting a pointed finger at the camera. Her face is tight, jaw set, and there's a defiance in her expression that most victims, in Evie's experience, never show. The girl is not hiding. If anything, she's daring the world to try again.

Evie copies the name into her spreadsheet and starts a search for 'Laney Jo Rayburn' and every possible spelling. Half an hour yields her entire digital footprint: the hospital bill GoFundMe, a Facebook account with privacy set to maximum, an arrest record for marijuana possession, and, finally, a Yelp review for a beauty parlor in Wichita Falls.

That's when it happens.

Evie is about to call the beauty parlor's main line to see if anyone answers, when the temperature in the room drops. She ignores it at first, until something moves into her periphery—a hand extends over her shoulder to point at the article photo.

She freezes to stare at it. The hand is there, but only a shimmer of reality. She turns slowly, expecting nothing. But then, her eyes could follow the arm up.

A man's face. Not reflected in the window, not visible in any real sense, but there in the sensation, the imprint of someone standing a foot behind her. The afterimage is so sharp she can almost taste his sports deodorant. It is the volleyball victim from this very town; she realizes—Lawrence Holloway.

His presence is not angry or accusatory. It is desperate.

The ghost hand, if it could be called that, points to the laptop screen. At Laney Jo.

"Her?" Evie whispers.

The presence surges, then flickers, then fades to a cold weight at the base of her skull. It is an answer.

Evie sits for a minute, letting the sensation bleed away. She re-reads the article, scans the photo, searches for meaning. Lawrence wants her to see Laney. Maybe not just as a data point, but as a person. A survivor.

She says into the empty room: "You want me to go to her, don't you?"

Nothing. The room is just a room again.

Shaking her head, Evie copies Laney's contact info into her spreadsheet. Wichita Falls is a solid day's drive from here.

She pivots, attempting logic on a problem that is anything but logical. Why would the spirit care about a kidney theft? Unless the Texas case is the template—the dress rehearsal before the main event, now repeated with fatal confidence in Missouri and elsewhere.

But then, Laney survived. That would explain why Lawrence is so insistent.

Evie sits back, breathing hard, her heart hammering with a combination of adrenaline and something close to wonder. She's seen a thousand case files. She's written hundreds of victimologies. But having an informant from the other side... *Uh, yeah.*

Evie stares at the ceiling, then says, "Fine. I'll go."

She kills the lights, leaving the laptop open for the next morning. As she plops down onto the polyester bedspread, she can't help but wonder about this specter, the way he hovered without malice. Will he follow her to Texas? Might there still be others?

Either way, she has her next step.

She is not afraid, at least not in the traditional sense. But as she drifts off, she finds herself scanning the darkness, looking for any sign—however faint—that she's headed in the right direction.

And for once, she almost believes she is.

Evie wakes before sunrise. Crashing early leads to rising early. The cheap blanket is static-charged and sweat-damp. Her back muscles complain from the mattress's central trough.

The shower is tepid but clean; the mirror, after she wipes away the fog, shows a face only slightly more haunted than the night before.

Evie dresses, repacks her bag, and checks the laptop for messages. No new emails. No otherworldly interruptions. She half expects Holloway to appear, or Janes from the crosswalk, but the only presence in the room is her own fatigue.

At the front desk, the day clerk has swapped in for the YouTube addict. Evie hands over her keycard, and he asks, "Was the room all right?"

She gives a thin smile. "It worked."

He offers a donut from the box on the counter. "Long drive ahead?"

"Texas."

He whistles, eyes wide. "Better grab two."

Evie thanks him, takes both, and heads outside. The morning is shrouded in fog; the streetlamp halos blurred into nothing. She throws her bag in the backseat, climbs in, and starts the car. The radio, still set to public news, drones quietly about a cold front sweeping south. She ignores it, focusing on the trip ahead.

It's almost ten hours to Wichita Falls. She could make it straight through, but part of her wants to pause, to tie off the unfinished thread with Hayes before she's out of range.

She waits until she's merged onto the interstate, then grabs her phone at a rest stop and composes a text.

> EVIE: You didn't deserve a haunted lunch. Glad you could roll with it. I'm heading out. Shift in plans. If I make it back this way, how about I buy your coffee next time?

She hesitates, then adds...

> EVIE: Seriously. You made a difference.

She hits send before thinking better of it.

The reply comes quicker than expected.

> HAYES: I'll hold you to that. Stay sharp, pro-filer.

She smiles for real this time. The road stretches out before her, sun burning off the last of the fog. Evie adjusts the mirror, catching her own eyes—brown, tired, but with a new glint behind them. The world is uncertain, haunted, full of wounds that spill out stars.

But the spirits imply there are answers ahead. And that, at least, feels like progress.

She presses the accelerator, windows down just enough to let the cold in, and drives south, whatever ghosts—friendly and otherwise—can ride shotgun.

Chapter Thirteen

Laney Jo

The strip mall looks the same as a thousand others: a nail spa, a payday loan, a vape shop, then the hair salon with its hot-pink scissors glowing against the dusk. Evie parks at the far end, under a billboard that promises low-cost cremation and a discount with every pre-pay. The lot is empty except for a matte-black pickup and a battered Camry with Oklahoma plates.

By the time Evie reaches Wichita Falls, the sun is nearly down, but the windows are still bright. Inside, the overhead lights brilliantly highlight all the styling chairs, hairdryer domes, etcetera. Evie lingers outside a beat, studying the contours: four chairs, two stations, a waiting area flanked by racks of salon shampoo. A "CLOSED" sign dangles from a suction cup. The last customer is halfway out the door, a silver-haired lady carrying a perm so tight it practically squeaks.

The stylist behind the counter is Ms. Laney Jo Rayburn. Blonde braid, olive skin, biceps the envy of any rodeo queen. She's wiping down her tools, forearms taut, inspecting the steel shears. There's a quality to her movement—practiced, as equally at home with blades and likely as sharp with small talk.

Evie taps on the glass. Laney looks up, frowns, then points to the sign: CLOSED.

Evie holds her ground. The move is calculated; she knows how a certain kind of person responds to persistence. Laney stares a second, then shrugs, flips the lock, and cracks the door three inches.

"You lost?" Laney says, with a voice that expects the answer to be yes.

"Looking for Laney Jo," Evie replies.

The door opens the rest of the way. The inside scents of hairspray, and a faint note of coconut oil. Up close, Laney's features are sharper than the internet suggested: high cheekbones, nose freckled and slightly crooked, a single gold stud piercing one nostril.

"Is this about the Yelp coupon?" Laney hikes an eyebrow. "Because that's just a scam by my ex."

Evie shakes her head. "I'm not here for a cut."

A slow, evaluating glance. "Well, that's a damn shame. I could do a lot with those curls." She gestures at Evie's head. "You ever let a professional have at that, or you just wake up like a cartoon sheepdog and call it a day?"

Evie's mouth quirks. "Natural is low maintenance."

"Not from this side of the chair, it isn't."

A silence, then Laney continues: "So what is it? You lookin' for a job? Or just here to case the joint? My money's on the latter, since you parked three stores down and walked up like you didn't want anyone to see you."

Evie crosses her arms. "You ever get a visit from a rag journalist? Maybe a PI? Anyone sniffing around your—"

Laney snorts. "Sweetie, I've had more creeps in the last year than a Dollar General on Black Friday. The day I woke up short a kidney, the only person who believed me was my own damn horse. You gonna try and do better than that?"

Evie is prepared for the defense, but not the humor. It throws her, in a good way. She can't stifle her chuckle. "I just want to ask a few questions."

"You a cop?"

"Not anymore."

Laney leans forward, rests one hand on the glass door. "You the Feds?"

Evie smirks. "Not anymore," she repeats.

For the first time, Laney's suspicion softens. "Well, shit. If you're not here to drag me back to Fort Worth, or force me into a cult deprogrammer show, you must really be bored."

She steps back, waves Evie inside.

"C'mon, before the landlord shows up. He's not a fan of my over-time."

The place is cleaner than Evie expects; the tools are aligned obsessively. Laney wipes her hands on a shop towel, then leans against the counter, legs crossed at the ankle. Evie notes the boots—scuffed but cared for, brown leather, the soles worn on the outside edge.

"Want a drink?" Laney asks. "I got a flask under the register, but we'll have to pretend it's cough syrup for insurance purposes."

"I'm driving," Evie says, gratified by the way Laney's lips curve into a brief, almost involuntary smile.

Laney gestures at the chairs. "Sit, or are you one of those who needs to pace to process?"

"I'll stand."

"Suit yourself."

Laney gauges her, eyes narrowing. "You don't look like you need protection, but you sure as hell don't appear to measure up to trouble."

Evie shrugs. "You'd be surprised."

The silence that follows is not hostile, just electrically charged. Evie feels a kind of mirrored energy—two animals waiting to see who blinks first. She takes the first step.

"The man who died in Missouri—Lawrence Holloway. He was missing his organs. The wound pattern was familiar to me."

Laney's face goes still, all the humor drained at once. "Yeah, I heard about him. You think it's the same one?"

Evie nods. "I considered you might be the test run. Or at least, you were meant to be. But you survived."

"Damn straight, I did," Laney says, with a flicker of pride. "Wasn't gonna let some Ruskie psycho make a lampshade outta me. Still got both lungs and the liver to prove it." She lifts her shirt a half-inch to show the fading scar—white, jagged, bisecting her right oblique.

Evie flinches. "That's not typical for a black market. Usually, it's clinical."

Laney barks a short laugh. "What, you think I'm not good enough for the real traffickers? Had to get the B-team?"

Evie smiles. "Not what I meant."

"Sure it isn't." Laney leans forward, voice dropping. "You mind telling me why you care so much? Because unless I missed the trend, most ex-Feds don't bother with charity cases."

Evie hesitates. The truth is complicated, and she can't give all of it, so she offers a sliver. "There are patterns. Sometimes they bleed over. You were one. The man in Missouri was another. There's a third, but I haven't tracked it yet."

Laney nods, as if she already guessed. "Let me guess: all of us got a nice clean donor card in our wallet?"

"Either that, or your blood tops the charts at a Red Cross drive."

"I got O-neg. Universal donor." Laney says this like it's a punchline. "Always figured if the end of the world came, I'd be the first one on the menu."

Evie studies her, sees the fatigue in the eyes, the long fuse of anger that's never quite burned out. "You want to help me find the guy?"

Laney raises both eyebrows. "You get that if I say yes, I might be putting a target on my back?"

"Who's to say there isn't already one there?"

For a second, neither speaks. Then Laney breaks: "Damn. You're good at this. Even the therapists can't keep me on the hook for more than five minutes."

"I'm not a therapist."

"Yeah, but you got the stare." She mimics it—eyes wide, jaw tight. "Like a chess robot."

Evie grins, which feels odd. "Maybe."

"Okay, chess robot. Here's the deal. I just finished a shift and have some tips to count, but if you want to play detective, you buy the first round. There's a bar down the street that does pitchers and karaoke. Just don't expect me to sing."

Evie agrees with only a tilt of her head.

Laney grabs her bag, flicks off the overheads, and shoulders past her toward the door. "You need to use the ladies' before we go? Now's your chance."

Evie shakes her head.

The air is cool, the sky bleeding from blue to purple. A half-moon hangs over the strip mall, the parking lot lit by security bulbs. Laney locks the salon door with a sharp twist, then gestures at the empty street.

"C'mon. You want to avoid the night weirdos, we better beat the shift change."

They set off side by side. Laney walks with the confidence of someone who knows all the shortcuts and any threats within a mile radius. Evie matches her stride, but keeps a half-step to the right—habit.

"So, what's your story?" Laney asks.

Evie considers how much to reveal. "I was an FBI profiler. Serial homicides, then financial crimes. Now I'm between jobs, you could say."

"Is that like in the shows? You got the big board and the red yarn and the crazy eyes?"

"Sometimes."

"Huh." Laney mulls this over. "You ever catch any?"

Evie's mouth tightens. "A few. Sometimes we just stop them. Sometimes they don't."

"Well, if it helps, I think you're the first Fed I've met who doesn't smell like crullers and Old Spice."

"That's probably because I'm under five-foot-two. They don't issue the Old Spice until you make field supervisor."

Laney cracks up. "Hell yeah. Short squad."

They keep walking. The avenue is busy now, headlights stretching into the distance, but the sidewalks are clear. Laney tells a story about the first time she roped a calf at age nine, how the damn thing flipped her on her ass but she still finished the loop.

"Point is," she says, "pain's just another word for 'not dead yet.' You figure that out, you're already ahead of the game."

Evie likes the philosophy. It's more honest than most.

They reach the bar. LEDs scroll 'COLD BEER & BILLIARDS.' Evie can hear the thrum of country pop from inside, the rise and fall of a crowd already one round in. Laney pauses at the door, turns to face her.

"You sure you're good?" she says, suddenly serious. "I mean, I'll cover your six if you cover mine, but these people... They eat outsiders for breakfast."

Evie says, "I'll take my chances."

"Okay, then." Laney glances up and down the street, then back at Evie. "Let's get weird."

The door swings open. Warmth and noise spill out, and for a second, the world feels almost like any other night, any other place. They stand at the threshold, two survivors, neither quite sure what they're about to step into.

But for now, it's enough that they're side by side.

Laney grins, and leads the way in.

Chapter Fourteen

Toasts & Tattoos

The bar is a world apart from the order of the strip mall. Inside, everything leans amber: booths glow with ancient, sticky varnish; overheads flicker through cigarette haze, though smoking's been outlawed since the Obama years. Near the pool tables, three off-shift EMTs argue about football. At the bar proper, a bearded man in denim performs a solo exorcism on a tray of hot wings. There are TVs, but none tuned to sound; even the music is subdued, as if the staff knows the customers only come for cheap drinks and uncritical company.

Laney makes a beeline for the corner booth, the one with the best view of every exit and the register. She gestures for Evie to follow, then flags a waitress with two fingers and a "We'll take the pitcher, sweetie. Whatever's lightest." The waitress, maybe forty, maybe seventy, gives Laney a wink.

Evie slides into the booth, her bag to her right, jacket draped carefully over the seat. She catches her reflection in the mirrored wall and, for a moment, sees herself as a stranger would: small, the only one in the room who isn't built for hard labor or hard drinking. She smooths the napkin on the table, folds it in half, then again into quarters.

"Let me guess," Laney says. "You're one of those who can't stand crumbs on the table, but you'll eat gas station jerky with your bare hands on a road trip."

Evie shrugs. "Messes are fine, as long as I make it."

The pitcher arrives with two frosted mugs. Laney pours with one hand, eyes still scanning the room, and slides the first glass to Evie. "To surviving," she says.

Evie raises the mug. "And to whoever keeps the lights on in these places." She sips. The beer is bland, almost watery, exactly right for the context.

Laney eyes her over the rim. "So. You gonna tell me why you came all the way to Wichita Falls to look up a washed-out rodeo queen with only one good kidney?"

Evie leans back. "Just running down theories. Gave me an excuse to buy a hat while I'm here."

Laney's mouth tightens, but not in anger. "You know, a hairdresser don't need to read the news, lady. It all comes pouring out in the shop. Go on. Tell me."

Evie waits. In every interrogation, there's a point where the other party wants to talk. They just need the room. She can see it already—the way Laney's jaw ticks, the way her boots bounce in place, the way she keeps glancing at Evie's hands, as if expecting them to twitch or reveal a tell. Classic survivor: doesn't want to show pain, but dying to be believed.

"You ever wish you could remember less?" Evie says.

Laney snorts. "Every damn day. Trouble is, the less you want to remember, the more it sticks. Like a tick on a dog."

Evie smiles. "Funny, isn't it? The human brain can filter out everything except what makes you want to jump off a bridge."

"You in recovery?" Laney asks, not unkindly.

Evie shakes her head. "Not for that, no." She sips. "But I know the look."

Studying her for a second, Laney relaxes an inch. "Fair enough."

They drink in silence. The jukebox shuffles through a medley of classic country—Patsy Cline into Garth Brooks, then a lurching segue to Taylor Swift. The crowd near the pool tables grows, but nobody pays attention to their booth.

After a hot minute, Laney says, "You really want the story, or do you just need to fill a file?"

"Neither," Evie says. "I'd rather figure out what you know you don't think is worth saying."

Laney considers this. "Most people just want the highlights. The gory details."

Evie leans in. "Try me."

Laney wipes foam from her lip, stares at her mug. "Okay. But I'm warning you, I've told this to a hundred reporters and a dozen lawmen. And all I ever got was a thicker case file and some Bible tracts in the mail."

Evie gestures, inviting her to proceed.

"First off, I wasn't drunk," Laney says, jabbing the table with a solid finger. "They like to say that, but I wasn't. I got off work, went home, and the guy was hanging out by my house. Seemed cute enough, I was being neighborly. It was only after I got drugged that he really opened up. Guy must've watched me for days. He knew where I parked, when my roommate left town, even what brand of soup I had in the cabinet."

Evie says nothing.

"He was calm. Not like the movie creeps. He talked to me for a full two minutes before he did anything. Said his name was Alex. He even offered me a cigarette, like it was a meet-cute in a bad romance.

I remember thinking he was good-looking, but in a way that's almost too much—like a news anchor or a politician's kid."

Evie takes a mental note: sociopath, probably high verbal IQ, likely practiced.

Laney continues: "He asked if I'd ever heard of the 'Deliverer.' I thought he was kidding, like it was a gang name. But then he said he was the Deliverer, that I'd be asleep for most of what happened, and that he hoped I'd wake up. For closure, he said."

"Closure," Evie echoes.

"Yeah. I didn't believe it until I woke up in the tub, half-naked and taped at the wrists. There was blood everywhere, but none of it was on the floor. All the drains were running, and the note on the mirror said, 'You're special. Keep going.'" Laney laughs, sharp. "Can you believe the balls on that guy?"

Evie nods, lets the silence hang a second. "You ever figure out why you?"

Laney pours herself a half glass, slowly. "Like I said, I got O-negative. Universal donor. Never shut up about it, even had it on a T-shirt in high school. They say he—whoever 'they' is—targets people like that. Young, healthy, perfect labs. I'm guessing if you're lucky, you wake up like me with a scar. If you're not, you end up in a ditch. Not just a news headline."

"Do you recall his face?" Evie asks.

"Hell yeah," Laney says, "but it didn't help. The cops drew a sketch. You want to see?"

Evie nods. Laney reaches for her bag—a small, battered messenger with a "Screw Cancer" patch—and produces a folded newspaper clipping. She slides it across the table. The sketch is sharp: a man in his thirties, severe jaw, short brown hair, eyes like they're bored with everything.

Evie studies it, then looks back up at Laney. "Do you mind?" She whips out her phone and holds it over long enough for her drinking pal to nod. Then, she snaps a flash with her camera. "Thanks."

"Don't thank me. The cops said it's a dead end. Too many people fit that look, nobody wants to testify, and the only time the Sheriff came down, he just took notes and left. Case is colder than my grandma's pot pie."

Evie leans back, letting the words settle. She wonders, not for the first time, what would happen if she told Laney about her own stalkers, the way the Harbinger speaks through dead men and visions. She doesn't, but the urge is there.

Instead, she says, "Have you been contacted since? Threats, phone calls, people following you?"

Laney shakes a denial. "No. But you're not the only one asking." She leans in. "A few weeks after, I got a visit from two guys. Military type. Special Forces. Not local law. They asked weird questions. Wanted to know if I remembered the guy's shoes. His watch. Even the way he wore his jacket."

"Special Forces?" Evie asks, surprised at their interest.

Laney shrugs. "You bet. They had tattoos, matching ones. Looked like a skull with wings. I saw it only when they pulled out their wallets for our lunch."

Evie notes it. "Why would ex-military care about black market organs?"

Laney laughs, low. "Maybe they were shopping. Maybe they're trying to keep my good stuff off the street."

Evie feels the pieces shift, slotting into a new grid. Could this Deliverer just be the errand boy for a bigger machine? She almost says it out loud, but stops. Instead, she asks, "Do you ever wonder what happened to your kidney?"

Laney looks at her, a flicker of something raw beneath the armor. "Every time I wake up hungover, I do."

Evie smiles.

They sit in silence. The pitcher nearly empty. Their pool table crowd is thinning, the EMTs down to one who nurses a single glass and watches the weather channel on mute.

Evie thinks about what to say. She could tell the truth—that she is here for justice, just maybe not the court-appointed sort. That maybe she's chasing a ghost, or maybe the ghost is just what's left after too many unsolved cases eat through your boundaries.

Instead, she asks, "You want to help me chase it down?"

Laney's answer is instant. "Hell yes. I'd pay good money to have my opportunity. Even better if I get to kick him in the balls for a solid hour."

"Deal." Evie grins. "Would you mind if I took a DNA sample?"

Laney blinks, then cracks a sharp grin. "What, you want a piece of me already? Most guys at least buy dinner first."

Evie returns the smile, subdued. "It could help. There's a forensic angle."

Without hesitation, Laney digs in her purse, rooting past a tangle of receipts and an inhaler, and pulls out a battered hairbrush. "How much you need, doc?" She plucks a few strands, golden and wiry, and offers it between thumb and forefinger.

Tearing out a sheet from her notepad, Evie folds the hairs into the makeshift envelope, and pockets it.

They sit, two survivors with nothing but scars and an empty pitcher of light beer. The world outside the bar is dark, and likely getting colder, but for now, the booth is warm, and the potential of an answer—however vague—lingers between them.

Evie finishes her beer, then stands. Laney does the same, stretching out her back and wincing at an old injury.

As they leave, Laney says, "You know, you could use a trim."

Evie smirks. "Maybe next time."

"Just saying. You want to blend, you gotta look the part."

Evie nods, and for the first time in a long time, feels almost ordinary.

They step into the night. Laney heads for her battered Camry, Evie for the Fiesta, the streetlamp flickering like a nervous tick.

There is a sense—fleeting, but real—that the two of them have just agreed to something much larger than beer and war stories. Maybe they're already in it. Maybe they've always been in it. Either way, it beats being alone.

Evie starts the car, hands steady on the wheel, and for the first time in months, does not check the rearview for ghosts.

Chapter Fifteen

Monk Hunt

Cole hits Oakland with the sky trying for sun but choking on its own exhaust. The city is a maze of new bones stacked on old—gentrification by way of amnesia, glass and steel cantilevered over blackened brick and graffiti that no one pretends to see. Rhys navigates from the passenger seat with his boots up and his head on a swivel, taking in the ruined splendor of Telegraph Avenue as if it's a crime scene only he can read. Cole prefers to drive. With hands at two and ten, muscle memory never dies.

The target is a five-story antique on the edge of downtown, all art déco curves above and plywood patchwork at ground level. Officially, it's a coworking hub called "The Deck." Unofficially, it's a haven for the kind of freelancers who live off burner phones and cash in envelopes, the city's parasite class. They park two blocks away, close enough to respond, far enough not to show up in every security frame.

They're hunting a guy called HeapMonk, which is not even the worst handle Cole's heard, and Rhys won't shut up about it.

"Bet you five bucks he's got a Hot Pocket in his hand and anime on loop when we breach," Rhys says, knuckles tapping out Morse on the wheel. He wears mirrored aviators, though it's well past dark, and the only reflection is neon strip and blue dashboard.

Cole's reply is flat. "I want it done in under three minutes." No inflection, no room for banter. He checks the holster under his jacket, thumbing over the retention snap.

Rhys grins, coyote-bright. "You're such a romantic, Danner. Don't you ever just wanna savor the job?"

Cole doesn't answer. He's reviewing the file in his head: Heap-Monk, aka Chester John Rinehart. Age thirty-six, skipped two years of college before vanishing into the Tor pipeline.

Evidently, one of their CEOs' resort villas in Virginia burned its way into a slagged crater last week. They needed to know how it had been discovered. Digital forensics back at the corporate shop traced an IP hop to this exact block, courtesy of a slip-up in something called StackOverflow syntax. The guy's mistake: answering his own forum question from a burner that wasn't as clean as he thought. Mercer's crew pounced, then sent in Rhys and Cole as the human mop.

"Showtime," Rhys says, and fishes a small wedge of gum from his pocket. He offers one to Cole, who declines.

They move as a unit, unspeaking. Cole at point, Rhys trailing with the tactical flashlight palmed but not lit. The vestibule reeks of old weed and possibly oven cleaner, maybe meth. Cole keys in the entry code from the dossier. The door gives with a dry groan, and the first step inside is a blackout: just a thin landing and a switchback to the stairs.

"Camera at ten," Rhys murmurs.

Cole spots it. Old Axis model, the dome is smudged and cheap, but the IR lens glints even in darkness. He scans for power; finds it. Not worth the risk of tripping a silent alarm or broadcast. He pulls his ball cap lower and keeps moving.

Second floor: the co-working space. A historic building, converted for tech nomads, open twenty-four hours but closed to the public after six. Their mark, according to the file, is subleasing from a "wellness start-up" that didn't survive the Delta variant. All the furniture in the common area is the IKEA kind that lasts exactly two years before surrendering to gravity.

Rhys sniffs. "Guy's a mouth breather for sure. You see the burrito wrappers?"

Cole catalogues: seven in sight, all Chipotle, all staked in an even line along the windowsill. Each wrapper is rolled tight, not balled. Odd detail, but maybe important later.

At the end of the hall is a door labeled: "Quiet Only Beyond This Point." No names.

Rhys angles right, prepping to breach. "Take bets on whether he's pants-on or off?" he whispers.

Cole ignores it. He listens. Behind the door: a faint click, then a whine, something like a cooling fan on its last leg. He signals: two fingers, entry on three.

They hit the door together. Cole's shoulder, Rhys's boot, then the sound of a frame splintering and the slide of something heavy knocked over. The room is a cave, lit only by three monitors in a crescent, the glass glowing blue and migraine-bright. No sign of HeapMonk, but there's a heat in the air, the kind of static you get when someone has just left.

Cole steps in, weapon drawn. Rhys sweeps the left, then curses under his breath.

"Out the window," Rhys says, then, "Jesus, what a mess."

Cole sees it: open sash, and a flex tube—a yellow plastic trash chute, rigged from window to the ground for construction refuse, but just big enough for a human to squeeze. There's a trail of static-cling

Cheetos and a dropped phone. Cole hears a rattle from outside, the sound of someone landing hard, then sprinting.

"Go!" Cole says, and Rhys is already vaulting the sill, sliding down the tube like a luge.

Cole doubles back, takes the stairs three at a time, heart rate steady, breathing shallow. At ground level, he bursts through the fire exit, just in time to see Rhys in pursuit: HeapMonk has mounted a dirt bike, two-stroke engine blaring, and is fishtailing down the alley. Rhys curses again, gives a half-hearted chase, but it's a lost cause after twenty yards.

"Damn it!" Rhys yells. "Should've checked for backup wheels."

Cole doesn't respond. He sees the streak HeapMonk left behind—a trail of blood on the trash tube lip, and the sense-memory of a body moving fast enough to miss the foot pegs.

Back inside, Cole examines the room. The heat from the monitors still radiates. He sweeps for signs of return—sometimes the really dumb ones double back, hoping to rescue their hard drives, or maybe their dignity.

Instead, Cole finds only the aftermath: monitors cycling through screensavers, a battered gaming chair upended, and, by the chair, a small, quivering terrier. The dog's eyes are wide, and there's a moment where Cole wonders if the thing will bite, or bolt, or just piss itself. He crouches low.

"Hey, buddy," Cole says in the gentle voice that used to work on rural Afghan kids. "You got a name?"

He checks the collar: "Zork." Of course. The dog licks his hand, then retreats to a den made of old sweatshirts and Burger King wrappers.

Rhys is pissed, but not at Cole. "Want me to see if he stashed anything in the lot?"

Cole shakes his head. "Not yet." He catalogues: monitors, keyboard, the rat's nest of external drives and USB dongles on the folding table. There's a half-assembled AR-15 upper on the desk, with a 3D printed lower. Probably for show, but you never know. He finds a Polaroid in the drawer: HeapMonk, smiling in a party hat, arms around two people—one is blurred with digital smudge, the other is a woman with shaved sides and a septum piercing.

Rhys circles, peeks over Cole's shoulder. "Family or just a party?"

"Doesn't matter." Cole's already pulling a roll of gaffer tape from his jacket. "Get the drives bagged. Sweep for any recording devices, security footage. Then torch the rest."

"Copy that," Rhys says, and starts unplugging with a speed that's almost elegant.

The terrier whines. Cole eyes it, then the little bed of trash it's curled in. He tries not to think about what it means that someone could flee a room and leave the only living thing behind.

They work in silence for six minutes. Rhys collects every scrap of silicon, then goes over the chair and desk with a can of accelerant from the 'wellness' office next door. Cole peels a backup battery from under the desk and tosses it into the tub, then sets a slow fuse from the window to the bin.

When it's almost done, Rhys says, "You want the dog, or you want me to?"

Cole turns. The animal is watching them, head cocked, tongue lolling with nervous energy. Cole kneels again, lets it sniff his fingers.

"Wouldn't want to miss an opportunity," Cole says. "The mark knows we were here, regardless. But he may be dumb enough to come back for the dog."

Rhys shrugs. "Woof. You sure are not going soft."

Cole gives a half-smile, almost genuine. "I prefer not to waste ammunition."

They stand at the threshold, double-check the scene, and then Cole flips the light switch. It does nothing—the place runs on motion sensors, and the sensors are all taped over—but the gesture is for closure.

They leave the pooch where he was abandoned. The accelerant starts its crawl along the tape, a line of flame moving slow and purposeful, just like the man who set it.

Outside, the city is unchanged. No sirens, no foot traffic. The homeless camp on the next block is already asleep.

In the car, Rhys tears open a new stick of gum and chews hard. "So what's next?"

Cole looks up at the windows of the building, scanning for the first sign of smoke. "We wait," he says. "If we move too fast, we miss the net. If we wait, the mark comes back for the one thing he cares about."

"The dog," Rhys says.

Cole nods. "The dog."

Rhys grins, a low rumble in his throat. "Never figured you for a pet lover, Danner."

"I'm not," Cole says.

He looks back up at the window, just as a faint orange bloom starts to pulse on the other side. Then, as if on cue, the terrier barks through the glass, sharp and rapid, a panic that echoes down the alley.

Cole closes his eyes, lets the noise play out, and waits for the next step. There's always a next step.

For now, he lets the quiet city wrap the car. He watches the little dog's silhouette, pacing behind the glass, and thinks of what it's like to be left behind.

Chapter Sixteen

What's Learned

There are motels in America that specialize in the art of making a traveler regret their choices. The "Willow Tree Inn" of Wichita Falls is such a place: walls the color of weak tea, a vending alcove that doubles as an echo chamber, bedspreads stitched in migraine-inducing geometrics. In Evie's room, the light is either full forensic or the strained dusk of a single lamp. She's spent the last hour alternating between the two, gauging case notes, trying to decide whether exhaustion is preferable to mild anxiety.

Her phone sits dead-center on the Formica table, screen-up and innocent. She's told herself not to check it for at least an hour. Maybe longer if her spiritual rider is in a foul mood.

It is not.

The text arrives at 9:11 p.m., polite as a dinner guest.

> LIAM: Hey. Sorry to bug you off shift, but you still among the living, Cross?.

Evie thumbs her reply...

> EVIE: Didn't know there was an on-shift. What's up, Detective?

Within seconds, three dots. Then...

> LIAM: Just wanted to confirm your safe landing. Also, got your tip about Rayburn. Doing some digging on my end now.

She smirks, picturing the man at his own kitchen table, probably typing one-handed, the other cupping coffee or a microbrew. She let him wait a full minute before answering.

> EVIE: Alive and intact. Motel is a step down from Quantico.

No reply for a while. She sets the phone down, goes to the bathroom, and splashes water on her face. The mirror is poorly mounted; the glass is thinner than her patience. She dries with a scratchy towel and reemerges to another ping.

> LIAM: Glad to hear. If you need backup, I'm ten hours up the road. Will bring pie.

She smiles, can't help it. Liam's style is methodical, a little dry, but it's there—a willingness to amuse, however deadpan.

Evie sits on the edge of the bed, thinking how best to proceed. There's the official angle—report progress, offer data, keep it strictly above-board. Or there's the truth, which is that she's pretty sure Laney was a "starter" victim. She floats it:

> EVIE: You ever see a run where the perp gets better at the cut after each case? This might be that. I'm thinking Rayburn wasn't some rando. She was first try, not the main event.

This time, the reply is instant.

> LIAM: Agreed. Never said it, but coroner's notes from MO suggest same. Were you able to get a sample from Rayburn? We could compare DNA. Any similarity.

She glances at the folded paper on her desk, the lock of pale hair twisted inside like a fortune cookie's warning.

> EVIE: Got it in my possession. You want it for analysis?

His return is a little slower this time.

> LIAM: If you're able to overnight, it'd be appreciated. More evidence is better, even if it's just a long shot. Address is on my card.

She gets up, roots through her bag for the card. It's standard issue, heavy cardstock, gold print: Missouri State Highway Patrol. Below, his cell, email, and the classic midwestern humility of "Detective" printed in a slightly smaller font.

> EVIE: Will ship tomorrow. You always this demanding with evidence?

> LIAM: Only when the witness is smarter than I am.

She snorts, stretches out on the polyester bedspread, and ups the ante.

> EVIE: How's Jefferson City this time of year? Worth a detour, or should I just mail it from here?

It's a throwaway, but he picks up.

> LIAM: JC is a tourist trap, unless you're into abandoned state buildings and meth heads. But if you swing through, I'll buy you better coffee than Lucky's.

She watches the typing bubble. There's another message coming, and this one is slower, more considered.

> LIAM: You mentioned before you didn't have family. No one waiting back east? Or just good at hiding your ring finger?

Evie stares at the ceiling, trying to decide if this is a real question or just detective banter.

> EVIE: Neither. Closest thing is a houseplant I left behind. And a couple ghosts.

She means it, but doesn't expect him to understand. Instead, Liam surprises her.

> LIAM: That tracks. I pegged you for a cactus person. The less it needs, the more you keep it alive.

She's not sure whether to be flattered or slightly called out.

> EVIE: What about you, Detective? You always work the late shift, or just couldn't let the case go?

A minute passes, then:

> LIAM: Both. Keeps my mind busy. Beats being home and thinking.

She wants to ask about his home, whether he's like her—chasing sleep from room to room, trying to solve things that won't stay solved. But she doesn't. Instead, she types:

> EVIE: I'll have the sample out in the morning. If you need anything before then, just text.

> LIAM: Will do. Weirdos love the motel strips. You be careful.

She laughs.

> EVIE: Pretty sure the real weirdos never leave the precinct.

This time, there's no reply. She wonders if he's gone to bed, or just lost in whatever files he's compiling.

She puts the phone facedown, then lies in the dark, listening to the building's skeletal groans, the mechanical wind of the HVAC. She tries to think of nothing, to let her mind idle. But it never does. After a while, she sits up, opens the curtains, and stares out into the lit-up parking lot. Her car sits where she left it, windows glinting. The lot is empty except for a white panel van and, across the chain-link, the familiar dead glow of a strip mall liquor store.

She almost misses it: movement, at the far side of the lot. A figure stands just at the edge of the light. She can tell by the stance that isn't quite right. There is no impatience, no hunch against the cold. Then it registers. It's the third one, red dress, torn t-shirt, auburn hair. The unnamed one.

Slowly pivoting on the sidewalk, her hands come to her chest to grip the torn edges of her t-shirt. The gesture is delicate, almost shy. She pulls them together, holding in the middle. The shirt reads "OKIE DOKIE" in blue, with a boot and hat, the kind they sell at truck stops along the turnpike. The same gaping wound ruins the woman's chest as before, but the blood is not fresh; it's more like a smear of ink. Holding the shirt closed, covering the wound, she then looks up—directly at Evie.

The motel window is cheap glass, and the darkness behind her is enough to make her own face the only real reflection. But she knows with absolute certainty what the message is.

Chicken-skin rises along her arms. It's not fear—she left real fear in another life—but a kind of awe, like the moment you realize the math problem is bigger than you thought.

She stands at the window. The ghost doesn't move. After a minute, Evie raises a hand, half-expecting nothing. The ghost mirrors her gesture.

Okay, she thinks. Okay. Next stop: Oklahoma.

She closes the curtain, locks the door, and, just to be sure, checks the closet and under the bed. No cameras, no peepholes, nothing but the expected stains and dust bunnies.

Evie strips to her base layers, sets an alarm, and kills the lamp. As she burrows under the stiff blanket, she glances once more at her phone.

No new messages, but the last one from Liam lingers at the top.

LIAM: You be careful.

Evie lies back and waits for sleep. When it doesn't come, she whispers to the darkness: "I'll bring pie."

The HVAC sighs, a cold exhale. Somewhere outside, someone waits for her to catch up.

In the end, that is comfort enough.

Chapter Seventeen

Mile 203

A hundred miles outside Wichita Falls, the sky is a raked plain of blue, perfectly wrong for the day she's having. Every leaf in Oklahoma has been stripped clean by the end of November; the light is so sharp it makes even the median grass stand to attention. Evie's Ford hums with the cracked rhythm of I-44. She lets it work on her, feeling each exit tick past in her peripheral vision.

She drives only a little outside the set speed limit—regulation, discipline, the old habits still in charge even if nobody else is. Evie cracks the window a smidge for a brisk, attentive balance and fresh air.

Time behaves differently out here. In the old days, a drive like this would be a puzzle: when to brake, where to fuel, how many miles before the next rest stop. Only now, with no way of knowing where she's going, no GPS, and no itinerary, every mile is just another increment. There's just a vague sense that she's on the correct path.

Hawks hover above the prairie, circling in search of random roadkill.

Left with the unending vista, her mind somewhat tends to chew at itself. The Cartographer case, the way it fell apart for their team. How she became an emptied husk of her former self in her own department afterward. She imagines how others at Quantico must talk about her now: Cross, the logic robot, the anomaly. Then there are the faces of the dead in her old folders, pixelated and wrong, which then overlays with those dead not in photos. The red dress, the OKIE DOKIE tee, the delicate way the ghost had gathered the shirt over the rent in her chest. The compulsion to follow.

She is no longer sure if this is grief, madness, or some new third thing.

Out of Lawton, she cuts northeast for Oklahoma City. The landscape is a slideshow—billboards for casinos, pro-life Jesus babies, tractor repairs, adult superstores with nothing in the lot but faded pickup trucks. In the distance, the wind turbines throw their arms skyward, spinning indifferently as the world under them stays stuck. She stops at a Love's for gas and jerky, ignores the man at the next pump who looks at her three times but says nothing.

Her impulse is to turn east at Oklahoma City, get lost in Tulsa, maybe head for the border and a real vacation. But the prodding in her ribs says no. It is a pressure, not a voice, a magnetic tug in her gut that does not allow for rerouting. She drives on, deeper, until the city's outer edges melt into rural haze and the signage goes from green and white to hand-painted and hopeful. The sky changes, too: at noon, the blue is so aggressive it aches behind her eyes. She fumbles in the glove box for sunglasses, and puts them on.

By now, the urge is almost physical. It's not a command, just a steady ratcheting of will, a sense that any deviation will be met with anguish—or worse. It is not the Harbinger, not exactly. She is learning to differentiate the flavors of these hauntings: the Harbinger is a cold flame, almost clinical in its logic. This is different. This is personal, pointed. The red dress, the Okie Dokie, the wound.

She merges onto I-35, heading north. It's the kind of stretch you see on disaster movies, nothing but scrub and drainage ditches, the road heat-warped and indifferent. There are no towns for fifty miles, only the faint promise of them at exit signs: Loyal, Hunter, Perry. The next service isn't for nearly an hour, but the sense of acceleration—something like gravity—pulls with each worn mile marker.

It happens just after 12:45 on a downslope near mile 203. The apparition is no hitchhiker at the edge of the shoulder. Even in daylight, the effect is jarring: the red dress is stark as a wound against the pale dead weeds, the woman's hair a banner in the windless air. She stands a half-step from the white line. There is nothing around her, no broken-down car, no suitcase, no shadow. Just that static, impossible figure and the certainty that she is meant to be seen.

Evie slows the car, not quite braking, but enough to make the speedometer uncertain. Her head turns, auburn hair flowing, as she nods, 'that way.' The woman is pale, her face unreadable, but the gesture is unmistakable. At the next sign—unincorporated, plus a name she can't pronounce—Evie turns off the freeway, guided by nothing but instinct and a specter of certainty.

The exit ramp circles under itself, narrowing to two lanes and then gravel. She feels the hairs on her arms stand up, a voltage not quite in the air, but in her bloodstream. This is what the Harbinger feels like: inevitability, an ache in her marrow. But this is also her choice.

At the bottom of the ramp, the apparition is waiting. Only now, she stands in the center of the access road, her arm still outstretched, pointing toward the weed-choked underpass. The sight is so wrong it feels like a movie error—a continuity goof in real time. The urge to keep driving, to avoid the moment, is almost overwhelming.

Evie pulls the car over anyway, kills the engine, and waits.

Nothing happens at first. No wind, no sound. The only motion is the ticking of the engine as it cools, a small clock counting down her resolve.

She waits for her pulse to subside, puts on her gloves, and then opens the car door.

The air is colder than before, raw as steel, and it cuts through the layers of her jacket as if she were bare. The ghost woman is gone, or at least, unseen. With a hesitancy to expect the unexpected, she walks toward the underpass.

The world here is empty. The fields are yellowed and stubbled; the road cracked and potholed; the embankment scarred with old run-off and junk. Evie steps over a length of wire, a plastic shopping bag, the flattened carcass of a frog. The only company is the crows, silent and watching from a row of fence posts.

She is nearly on the other side of the underpass when she feels the presence again—no longer visible, but absolute. The compulsion is not to look up, but to look down, into the ditch, fallow with high green grasses. She does.

Nothing. Just mud, trash, a few dried thistles, a drift of old leaves.

But the pressure persists.

She kneels, runs her gloved hands through the scrub, scraping at the frost-crusted detritus. For a minute, she feels nothing. Then: the edge of fabric, half-buried. It's the color that gets her—red, faded but not gone, the same as the dress in the vision. She tugs gently at first, then with increasing force. The earth resists, but yields.

There is a body.

Evie's brain tries to catalog the details, separate the real from the unreal. The remains are partial—months of exposure have done their work—but the proportions are unmistakable. No odor. The cold and exposure have seen to that. Her dress is bloodstained, the tee's torn words of OKIE on one side. Remnant strands of auburn are still attached to the skull.

Evie recoils, nearly losing her footing. The ground is soft here, the mud insistent. She breathes through the urge to vomit, her brain cycling through training: observe, assess, document. She checks for belongings, finds nothing. No jewelry, no wallet, just the ruin of a body and the faint, metallic taste of terror in the back of her throat.

Standing up, she backs away from the ditch, and looks at the underpass.

The ghost woman is on the embankment now, face turned away. She radiates sadness. The sense is of waiting—an unfinished story, a hand to her chin as if lost.

Evie turns, walks back to the car, and sits inside for a minute. The cold seeps through her jeans, into her bones. She thinks of the woman who raised her, to do the right thing, even if it meant breaking herself in half to do it. She thinks of the Harbinger, its unrelenting drive, and wonders...

Will there ever not be a need for this?

She takes out her phone, taps in her pin to unlock and—

Bang

Evie jumps, startled from her driver's side window taking a hit.

The auburn ghost woman is just there, staring back hard. Her eyes—serious but plaintive—as she slowly pivots her neck into a clear, 'No.'

Tucking her cell back into her coat pocket, the apparition fades with acceptance. And yet...

Oh, we're not done. This is not that simple.

Evie starts her Fiesta and pulls back onto the road, heading for the nearest town.

She spends the next hour on the move, orbiting a circuit of two-lane blacktops and abandoned access roads, double and triple-checking for signs of anyone following. There are none, of course, but routine is comfort. She pulls into the shade behind a deserted truck scale, eats her gas station jerky, and waits until her heart rate slows. By 3:05 she's back at the underpass, the pull irresistible and grim.

This time, she brings a notebook, a fresh pair of nitrile gloves, and a cheap disposable camera from a gas station. She parks, hidden by a low berm, and returns, hood up, head down.

The first rule of fieldwork: document, then disturb. Evie squats at the edge and runs a slow survey. The skeleton is mostly intact, still articulated by the remnants of tendon and ligament, but the soft tissue is gone, eaten by weather and wildlife. The dress is faded to a flag of red, the shirt's print just a whisper above the collapse of ribs. She takes photos from every angle, crouching low, getting the lay of the bone scatter. Three months' exposure, maybe four. No animal has moved the big pieces. That tells her something about the location. The killer expected her to be found, eventually.

There is no purse, no wallet, no phone. She notes this, sketches it on a page, then uses tweezers to retrieve a few strands of hair matted against the skull. Auburn, brittle, length five or six inches.

She paper pockets the sample, takes one more photo, then stands. The world is spinning, just a little. She blames it on dehydration, but there is a pressure building at the base of her skull. Not a migraine—this is the Harbinger's slow, cold iron pouring down her spine.

Evie turns, and the ghost woman is waiting at the foot of the embankment.

She's closer now, barely four feet away, the ruin of her chest hidden by her crossed arms. The face is hollow and moon-pale, but the eyes are bottomless, rimmed with an old sadness. The red dress is caked with earth, but the fabric does not hang as it should: it billows gently, as if moved by some unseen tide.

Evie's first instinct is to speak. Instead, she stands perfectly still, allowing the victim room for... whatever.

After a moment, the apparition takes a step forward, uncrosses her arms, and raises a hand—palm up, offering nothing. Her head tilts, slow, almost apologetically, and then she leans in. For a terrible instant, they are face to face, close enough that Evie smells a scent she can't place: not rot, not perfume, but something elemental. Petrichor, the memory of rain. Ethereal lips move, but the sound is lost. What comes instead is a shake of the head—slow, deliberate. No.

Evie wants to protest. She wants to ask out loud what it is she's not supposed to do. But the pressure builds, a cold hand at the back of her neck. The Harbinger understands her intent. Evie stares into the woman's hollow eyes and refuses to blink.

"I have to," she says, voice a whisper. "You know I do."

Her ghost hand drops. She turns away, steps up the embankment, and dissolves into the daylight. Not a fade, not a glitch—just the casual vanishing of someone who was never really there.

Evie exhales, lungs burning. She walks back to the ditch and kneels. Using a couple of sticks and a shred of an old grocery bag, she fashions a marker, a flag above the grave. It's not a cross, but the intention is clear: here lies a person. Someone who matters.

Gathering her notes, she tucks the camera into her pocket, and brushes the dirt from her jeans. The wind picks up, rattling the roadside grass, and with it comes the first sound in an hour: a lone eighteen-wheeler, barreling down the overpass above, oblivious to the microcosm of loss beneath.

She walks back to the car, boots squelching in the mud. Standing before the trunk, she strips off her nitrile gloves and tosses them inside. Leave nothing behind. Old habits, hard to break. The chill lingers, but her hands are steady.

The nearest Greyhound stop is twelve miles north, on the kind of main street that survives only by inertia. She pulls into the lot, parks, and walks to the payphone at the corner. It's covered in stickers and grime, but she's seen worse. She fishes two quarters from her jeans, lifts the receiver, and dials for state police. This entity doesn't want her to make this call, so she should at least do it anonymously.

As the line rings, Evie glances across the lot. The sun is sinking behind a low cloud, the sky a haze of pink and gray. She thinks of the girl in the ditch, the one who just wanted to be seen. Then of the Harbinger, and whatever rule she's about to break.

She waits for the operator's voice, hand tight on the receiver.

Sometimes, you don't get to decide. Sometimes, you're just the last one left to call it in.

Chapter Eighteen

Small Comforts

It is dusk when Evie crosses back into Missouri, the last light receding behind her like an afterthought. The interstate is an endless ribbon of chilled asphalt, bracketed by fields too flat and bare to even feign mystery. Another two and a half hours later, Jefferson City materializes at the edge of a Stuckey's sign. It's the kind of place that makes few promises and delivers even less. Evie takes the exit anyway. There's comfort in its banality: a Walmart, a car wash, three competing churches, a chain motel.

The two hair samples—one from the mortuary in Ohio, the other from the ditch in Oklahoma—are tucked into separate envelopes, and in her bag. The third, a longer lock from Laney Jo, she'd FedEx'd ahead yesterday. Liam already texted he'd picked it up at the front counter, adding a 'Got the goods. Ping me next time you're in town.'

She wonders what exactly she expects the DNA will show? That the killer is pattern-driven, or that the pattern is recursive? That something more than chance links the victims? Maybe she just wants the certainty, a hard fact to hurl at the darkness, even if it won't matter.

Liam's place is what you'd expect: modest, a split-level with vinyl siding, a pickup in the drive, porch light already on. She walks up, feeling the nerves, not for the case but for what comes after—the explanations, the questions, the probability of having to justify the haunted look she can't quite scrub from her face.

He opens the door on the first knock, in jeans and an ancient Royals sweatshirt. The house smells like onions and pepper, and behind him, the noise of a game filters in from the TV.

"Evening, profiler," he says. There's a smile, but only just there.

"Evening, Detective," she counters, stepping past him into the foyer. The air is warmer here, and she lets herself settle, boots leaving a faint trail of road salt on the tile.

Liam produces the FedEx package, waving it. "Picked this up early, wasn't expecting such a rapid follow up. You could have brought it yourself after all. Have another change of plans?"

She shrugs. "That's one way to put it."

He leads her to the kitchen, which is far neater than her own.

Evie slides her two additional paper envelopes across the counter. "You can include A and B now, as well. I'd like them checked against the Texas sample. No chain of custody, but they're clean."

Liam's eyebrows lift. "What? We're adding a double-blind test as well? I mean, I know the Texas woman. Who are these?"

She squeezes her lips into a frown. "I'm hoping you'll afford some latitude. Playing a hunch. Can explain later."

Not offended, he peeks into both envelopes, using slow, deliberate movements. "You know, when most people bring me mystery samples, it's from their cat's hairball or the neighbor's beard for a paternity thing."

"Would you consider me most people?" she asks.

He glances up, deadpan. "Absolutely not."

There is an ease to this, a rhythm. He is careful with the samples, careful with the way he looks at her. She leans against the fridge, watching him inspect.

"Usually takes a couple of days," he says. "Though if it's urgent, my department has access to a rapid DNA machine. The technician owes me from that time his dog swallowed a thumb drive."

Evie smiles, just a twitch. "No need to bend the rules. I trust you."

He washes his hands, then turns suddenly serious. "You all right? Sorry to say, but you look like you've not slept since you left."

She considers fibbing, then opts for the middle ground. "Travel takes it out of me. Had a pit stop in Oklahoma, which turned into a lot more than I planned."

He gestures to the living room. "Beer? Or coffee?"

"Beer," she says. "But only if it's local."

He returns in thirty seconds with two cold ones, hands her a bottle of something labeled in matte black. They settle in the living room, the DNA envelopes left behind in the kitchen.

There's a tension, but it's the good kind, the kind that means you're alive and someone sees it. The TV's on mute; the game's at halftime. Outside, the sky is sliding from blue to navy, and the windows reflect the two of them in faint outline.

"So what's the master plan?" he asks, half in jest. "You going to stick around until we get a result?"

She sips, savoring the first cold hit. "Might as well. Unless you've got a lead you're not sharing."

He feigns offense. "In that case, I might be tempted to snail mail these, Ms. Cross."

She nods and glimpses the grill just outside. "Are you game to barbeque?"

Liam looks surprised, then delighted. "Hell yes. I was about to fire it, anyway. Hope you don't mind chicken. Or the chef."

Evie stands, draining her bottle. "Just tell me where to set the table."

"Oh. Not on a night like this."

They head out to the deck, boots knocking against the worn wood. With the press of a button, he ignites the porch's tower heater. The amber glow presses back the falling evening. Liam's grill is ancient, possibly predating her own career, but its additional heat is immediate. He preps chicken and vegetables with the same precision as his sterile kitchen—seasoning in measured shakes, foil packets arranged like dossiers.

Evie collapses onto a plastic chair, knees up, watching his every move. She doesn't know why it's so easy to watch him, or why it feels like the right place to be. Maybe it's the fatigue, maybe the case, maybe the way the Harbinger has gone silent for the first time in days. She breathes in, lets the night air and the faint whiff of propane push away the memory of the woman in the ditch, the long miles, the grinding logic of the hunt.

Liam glances over. "You know, my ex used to say barbecue is the only time you see a real man cry."

Evie smiles. "What about funerals?"

He grins. "Not in my family."

She rolls another beer in her hands, playing with the beads of condensation.

"So what about you?" he asks. "Family?"

She hesitates, then shrugs. "Nothing left but me. Parents in Ohio, but I don't call as much as I should."

He nods, not pushing. "Sometimes that's for the best."

She wants to share more, to open the door on the stories stacked behind her chest, but she lets it lie instead.

The grill sizzles, and Liam flips the packets with a practiced hand. "You know, you're allowed to relax," he says, voice low. "Nobody's going to show up with a file and ruin the night."

She thinks of the Harbinger, of the last couple of weeks ruined by those compulsions, yet for the first time in a while, she almost believes him.

"Yeah," she says, voice barely above a whisper. "I'll try."

The silence is gentle, not loaded. Above them, the first stars push through the haze.

She finds herself wanting to believe in second chances. Or at least, in the temporary quiet that comes with good company, food, and the hope of comfort in a bottle, the way the world can sometimes slow down just enough for you to breathe.

She breathes.

And for a while, it's enough.

The grill hisses and pops, and every ten seconds or so Liam lifts the lid and prods the foil with the reverence of a man who knows his audience. Evie is that audience, though she does little more than lean into her jacket and clutch a second beer. He's playing a set, and she's not sure if she's supposed to laugh at the jokes or admire his technique.

When the chicken is ready, Liam shuffles it onto two mismatched plates, hands hers over with a practiced, one-handed maneuver.

"Hope you're not vegan," he says.

"Not anymore," Evie says. She waits a beat, then: "I lost faith in my twenties."

He snorts, opens a second beer for himself. "The Lord's Chicken never abandons."

They eat in parallel, neither making a move to fill the other's pauses. The chicken is peppered; the vegetables overcooked in places, but she likes that he didn't try too hard. The deck light casts everything in a sepia warmth, washing both their faces out to an old flickering film. It's almost perfect.

Halfway through her plate, Evie clears her throat.

"You ever wonder what happens to them?" she says.

He looks at her quizzically.

"The victims, I mean. Like, is there any universe where—I don't know—their awareness keeps going? After?"

He wipes his mouth with a paper towel, then folds it into a square. "You're asking if I believe in ghosts."

"Or souls. Or, hell, if there's anything left of a person once you drain out their body and bury what's left."

Liam purses his lips, considering the question as if it's an actual problem set. "I don't. Not really. But sometimes..." He trails off. "I think when something is so awful, it creates a kind of pressure that limps around."

"Like air trapped under a skin."

"Yeah." He drinks and then clutches his gut. "Like gas."

Evie laughs, but the sound is brittle. The Harbinger stirs, like the brush of a stiff wind along her spine. She pushes it out, letting the feeling pass. "You ever think you might've seen one? A ghost, I mean."

Liam shakes his head. "But I've seen people try to talk to them. I worked a case a few years ago—older woman, house full of weird smells and stranger noises. She'd lost a son in the Navy, and every night she swore he was in the attic, walking around." He shrugs. "Never found a thing. But I think she was happier believing he haunted her than accepting he'd been KIA."

"I get that," Evie says.

He cocks her a look, eyes searching for something more. "You've seen things, though. Stuff you can't explain. Right?"

Evie holds her bottle, knuckles pale. "All the time."

He lets her sit in it, neither mocking nor needing to rescue. "So what do you think is going on?"

She wants to say; They wait. They echo. They tap out messages on the inside of your ribcage until you can't tell which thoughts are yours. Evie wants to tell him about the crosswalk, the recurring apparitions, the Oklahoma hitchhiker who would not let her rest until the ditch was found.

Instead, she says, "I think the world is mostly noise. And once in a while, if you're unlucky, it can ring through with a clear signal."

He nods. "You think this guy—our killer—is mixed up in that?"

She starts to answer, but... her voice catches in her throat. A chill, sudden and absolute, grips her chest. Her hands go numb for a second. Her recognition is instant, that impossible cold, its intention: *Not now.* She is not to open up. *Don't.*

Evie blinks, and the sensation fades. She makes a show of sipping her beer, then pivots. "I think the killer is just a guy. Maybe smarter than most, utterly callous. But nothing else."

Liam's brow furrows as he leans back in his chair. "That's the answer that makes sleep possible."

"Not for me," Evie says, then, softer: "Not lately."

They finish their meal, neither hurrying nor prolonging it. The night thickens; the streetlights cast moth-shadows on the edge of the yard.

With the plates in the sink, Liam offers her another beer, but she declines.

"I'd better keep sharp," she says, glancing at her phone. "I still have to check into a motel."

"Worried about the night desk clerk?" Liam asks.

"Worried about a DUI," Evie says.

He grins, then stands, stretching his arms over his head. The gesture is almost comic, a Midwestern dad move, but it's deliberate, and she likes the way he fills the space.

They linger at the door, neither too sure how to wrap the night.

Liam says, "Decided to stick around until the DNA pops?"

She considers. "I don't have anywhere else to be. Besides, you've got better beer than most places."

He smirks. "I could slow-walk the results, buy us another dinner."

Evie raises an eyebrow. "Now, don't abuse the public trust."

"Is it, though?" he says. "If it brings about a greater good?"

She lets herself smile. "You're more philosopher than I expected."

He shrugs. "I did a year of community college. Philosophy 101, 'Introduction to Despair.'" Liam winks.

Evie likes the way he never goes for the easy joke, how he lets the awkward moments breathe rather than rushing to patch them.

She steps onto the porch, hands in her coat pockets. "I should go."

"Yeah," he says.

There is a beat where he almost... but then the moment passes. Instead, he opens the door, and she walks to her car. The engine is cold; the windshield is already fogged with dew.

As she starts the car, she sees him standing there, watching from the front porch. He's not waving, just making sure she gets off all right.

She drives. The roads are empty except for the occasional deer at the shoulder, glassy-eyed and dumb with hunger.

A mile off, her phone erupts—a staccato buzz, then another, then a whole chorus. At first, she thinks it's her old office, maybe. Something bad. But when she checks the screen at a stoplight, it isn't so simple.

Her phone is alive with notifications, all the apps blinking in frantic succession. Six new emails, fourteen DMs, three missed calls, and a dozen push alerts from services she barely uses. All the messages, regardless of platform, are variations on the same phrase:

EVIE, GOTTA TALK.

She's been hacked. More than that. This is a deliberate, coordinated signal. The kind of thing that would have made her laugh before, or call the IT desk, or just turn the phone off. But now, with the Harbinger's chill still in her veins, it feels different. Personal.

She pulls over, kills the engine, and flips through the messages. They are all signed, in their special way: Ethos. The air in the car is suddenly thin. She opens a window, lets the cold flood in. For a second, she feels an urge to throw the phone out the window, or maybe herself.

Instead, she types back:

EVIE: I'm listening.

The reply comes instantly.

CTRLZ: I knew you would.

In the dark, with the deck smoke still clinging to her hair and the taste of good beer on her tongue, she feels a tiny, bitter joy at the prospect of a next move. This is what she was made for, after all. Not comfort, not rest. Just the unending pursuit of something that can never truly be caught.

Chapter Nineteen

Ethos Activated

Evie doesn't answer CtrlZ's message right away. For a minute, she just sits in the driver's seat, watching the notifications stack up, each one coded to escalate: first a direct message, then a Discord ping, then three encrypted SMS in less than sixty seconds. Ethos has always been an impatient collective, but the speed here smacks of more than hacker anxiety.

She checks the mirrors, one hand on the wheel, half-expecting an unmarked car to appear in the lot. But there's nothing—just the glare of street lamps on the empty parking lot and, across the street, a bored clerk in the liquor store watching the world not end.

Fine.

She starts the engine and checks into a motel, the kind where the front desk partition doubles as a panic room. The night clerk barely glances at her license. He hands over a key card in a paper sleeve and gestures at the row: "112, down on the end, you're good." Then, to the silent TV, "Rain's coming," as if she needs to know.

The room is a box. There's a carpet so new it feels half tacky under her boots. Evie drops her bag on the bed and unzips the laptop with the urgency of a forensic tech.

She sits cross-legged on the polyester, boots still on, and powers up. The laptop is a battered ThinkPad, held together with decals and the last wishes of the U.S. government. Within seconds, the VPN tunnels her through four continents, then pings her into an onion-routed IRC channel labeled: //PHANTOM-TREAD//

CtrlZ is already there, spamming the chat with her trademark overkill:

> CTRLZ: Got a live one

> CTRLZ: Hop in, Agent

> CTRLZ: Time is short

Evie types:

> EVIE: I'm here.

A four-second lull. Then, as if they were waiting for that exact phrase:

> HEAPMONK: About freakin' time.

> ROOTMUSE: Had to be you.

> CTRLZ: Not the best news. Not the worst.

Ethos, in its full plurality, never fails to remind her that consensus is an arms race. But tonight the energy is ragged, less triumphant than cornered.

Evie sips the water from her travel bottle, then:

> EVIE: What happened?

A beat, then HeapMonk sends an invite... which approves itself.

Then in a blink, four windows tile up to fill her screen. There's a virtual avatar, a pixelated outline of a man that flickered between forms—sometimes glitchy, sometimes clean—labeled 'CtrlZ.' To his right, RootMuse's virtual self appears as a queen-of-diamonds but with a crown of code. But just beneath, a live feed of Evie pops up alongside a middle-aged scruffy guy in a hoodie. The username just under his: HeapMonk.

Well, there's a first.

"Had company tonight," HeapMonk says. His voice is staticky and raw, as if he's speaking through a mesh of tin cans. "Showed up at the Deck. Didn't even bother with subtle. Door got kicked in."

She waits for more, but he goes silent.

CtrlZ fills the gap. "Hey, Eve. Two military types, or ex. Gloves, no suits. Blackout kit, guns, the whole thing."

"They after you, or your drives?" Evie asks.

"Both. But mostly me, turns out," HeapMonk says. "They went through my stuff. They even got my dog, man."

RootMuse chimes in hot. "The frackers killed Zork!"

HeapMonk's breath hitches. "Left him in the room while they burned it down."

Evie closes her eyes. Zork, the terrier—she's seen in snapshots he's shared. She didn't know the dog, but she knew HeapMonk has no one else.

"How'd you get out?"

HeapMonk sniffles. "Construction chute. Dirt biked to the other side of town. Didn't even stop for shoes. Got the backup drives though."

CtrlZ's avatar buzzes visually. "Point being, they sent a message. It's not just us anymore. They know at least one of our faces now. How long before they crack the rest?"

"They know we helped you," says RootMuse.

Evie hears the underlying accusation but lets it slide. "Did you see their faces? Any insignia, tattoo, anything that stuck out?"

"Too dark. Didn't get a good look," HeapMonk replies. "One of them had a patch on his sleeve, but could have been fake."

Evie presses. "What kind of patch?"

HeapMonk pauses. "Skull. Wings. Like the old SF logo, but modern. Looked like what they wore in Afghanistan, maybe later."

She blinks, a memory surfacing. "You ever see a tattoo, same design?"

HeapMonk: "No clue. I was just hightailing."

"Why?" CtrlZ again. "What's the angle? We're nobody. We're just the middlemen."

Evie slows herself now, thinking of Laney, of the special ops guys in Texas with the skull-and-wings. "Your patch might match with a Wichita Falls attack last year. Kidneys for the black market, but the witness remembered it as a tattoo."

RootMuse pulls back his hood; his scraggly blond hair splays wild. "You think they're connected?"

Evie huffs. "Don't know. Shouldn't be. You guys weren't even helping me with this case. But does feel way too coincidental."

CtrlZ's avatar leans in. "Don't flatter yourself, profiler. We get threats every week. This is next-level. Someone wants a message sent, and only wants us alive long enough for others to read."

HeapMonk wipes his nose on his sleeve. "They're going after family. They're not after code, or cash, or hacks. This is personal."

RootMuse's code crown erupts in animated flames: "The dog."

HeapMonk adds, "Yeah. *My Zork.*"

"If you've got a still of the patch, send it," says Evie.

Absently, HeapMonk taps a few keys. "Already did. Uploading now."

A link appears in the chat, flagged [UNLISTED]. Evie clicks, and a compressed video file stutters into view: a blur of motion, a stairwell, then a frame-by-frame of two men hauling up the last flight. Hoodies obscure their faces, but the patch is clear enough—a winged skull, almost cartoonish, but with the precise geometry of a military patch. On one man's wrist, in the blue-white glare of emergency lights, is a partial tattoo of the same icon, dark as pitch against the skin.

"Yep," Evie says. "That's the one."

"I just want to hurt them," HeapMonk says, voice raw. "I want to hurt them so bad."

Evie nods. "You will. But you'll do it smart. No dead drops, no revenge porn, no wild crap."

He shakes his head. "I know. I just—Zork was a rescue. He didn't do anything."

RootMuse's queen sneers. "Everything is up for grabs now. Every node, every back channel."

Evie raises a finger. "Except this time, we can see the moves."

"You're assuming Mercer cares about loose ends," says CtrlZ. "If he's fielding black teams, it means there's something he doesn't want found."

"Maybe it's not a 'what,' but a 'who,'" says Evie.

A silence. The chat seems to contract, as if the processors themselves are anxious.

HeapMonk's voice: "You think it's about these new killings."

She purses her lips, considering. "I think the Cartographer case is not completely closed. I'm certain of Mercer's involvement, and I think he's using someone to keep everyone scared."

"Even us," says CtrlZ.

RootMuse's queen nods. "Especially us."

HeapMonk hikes up his hoodie, withdrawing into himself. "Then what do we do?"

"We don't panic," replies Evie. "Ethos shouldn't tip its hand. You each stay close to the bone, share nothing in the clear. And if they want a fight, they'll get one."

The three of them—two avatars and a man—go silent, each calculating the next move.

CtrlZ, as always, breaks the spell: "You ever think about why you keep at this, profiler? We know you walked. You don't owe anyone anything."

"I do. Or I did," Evie concedes.

Root's queen crosses her virtual arms. "You're not one of us, but you're not one of them either. That's why it works."

Evie logs out without ceremony.

She powers down, then lies back on the bed, staring up at the unmoving ceiling fan. The room is warm, but her core is cold. Evie waits for the Harbinger, for the familiar chill to spiral through her chest and freeze her thoughts. But it's quiet, utterly indifferent to what just transpired.

Why? She turns this over in her head, again and again, as she stares at the static white tiles above. Why is it okay to share the details with Ethos, when she can't even speak aloud to Liam or the people who once called her friend?

Maybe because, like her, they're already outside the system. What if the Harbinger knows that some truths only exist in the wild? Could be, the hope for closure might only lie in the hands of those willing to burn for it.

She closes her eyes, and waits for sleep.

Chapter Twenty

Lining Up Evidence

E vie wakes with the sense that someone else has lived her night for her. She checks the clock, expecting the usual 5:00 AM, but it's 10:47. The room is vivid: the thin strip of sun slicing under blackout drapes, her laptop on the desk, a coffee-stained notepad on the TV stand. The air is stale with the aftertaste of over-processed climate control.

She rolls over and spends a full minute staring at the orange light on the fire alarm. There's a weird stillness inside her—maybe the Harbinger slept in, too. She cycles through the night: the Ethos channel, a banged-up HeapMonk, the pixel-crown queen, and the chatroom's ceaselessness after she left. Nothing actionable in any of it, but the slow, non-negotiable draw toward a next move.

Except—she does not know what that move is. Since she started after this inner spirit, Evie could follow its breadcrumbs. Now, she feels the trail ahead of her flattening into a deserted plain.

She gets up, shuffles to the bathroom, and washes her face. Evie notes the micro-creases, the faint purpling beneath her eyes. She is beginning to resemble her mother, she thinks, but without the patience.

At 11:02, there's a knock on the door.

Her first impulse is to freeze. The second is to go for her Glock. But then, she's in Jefferson City, Missouri. Who would know she was here? Evie rises on her toes to spy through the peephole.

It's Liam.

Unchaining the door, she sweeps it open.

He stands half-turned, as if braced for a sudden blowback. His jacket is zipped against the late-November wind, but his face is composed, focused in the way of someone whose life is about to change.

"Morning," he says.

She glances at the sun angle, then back at him. "That's a generous interpretation."

He doesn't smile, but there's a fondness in his voice. "Can I come in a minute?"

She steps aside. Liam enters, carrying an insulated mug and a battered manila folder. He glances around the room—takes in the lack of clutter, the laptop on the desk.

"Wasn't sure if you'd be here," he says. "Didn't see your car out front."

Evie shrugs. "They made me park around the back. Some insurance thing. How'd you find me?"

Liam replies, "Not too too many motels in the area. This one was close."

He takes a seat at the small Formica table, sets down his coffee. For a second, Evie expects him to start the way her old Bureau bosses would—with the long, tight silence meant to invite confession. Instead, he thumbs open the folder, glances at her, and then at the closed curtains.

"How much sleep did you get?" he asks.

She considers. "Enough."

He watches her as if he's waiting for the real answer.

Evie sits opposite. She notes the folder: three labels, all in different colors. He slides it toward her, one finger tapping at the edge.

"Had the tech run your hair samples on the rapid kit first thing," Liam says. "Faster than standard. Got the results before I left."

She flips the folder open. The first sheet is a DNA sequence printout, all As, Ts, and Gs, bracketed by yellow highlighter.

"The Texas sample," she says, recognizing the name.

Liam nods. "Rayburn. Clean bill of health. Blood type O-neg, as she said. No red flags, no markers you wouldn't expect."

"Survivor profile," Evie says.

"Yep, next." He taps the second sheet. "Holloway, Missouri. This is where it gets strange."

She reads: Blood type A. HLA type matches what's listed in the old medical. But then, in the right margin, a note: 'Unusual allelic concordance to multiple submitted samples. Rerun advised.'

Evie looks at him. "What does that mean, exactly?"

Liam pinches the bridge of his nose, then takes a slug of coffee. "It means that if you didn't know better, and looked only at the traits, you'd think this hair and the next two could have come from the same person."

She scans the sheets. The Ohio sample—her Emily Janes—and the Oklahoma sample, labeled as "Jane Doe," both show nearly identical HLA markers to Holloway. The same rare alleles, the same secondary blood chemistry markers. Across three different people, three different states, and two genders.

Evie tries to calibrate. "You ran them twice?"

Liam nods. "Three times. The tech thought the machine was contaminated, so he did a full reset."

"And?"

"Nothing. Clean every time. The samples are different on other marks, but whomever they belong to—they are matches for these specific traits, at least at the loci that matter in order to transplant them."

She sits with this. In a way, it's exactly what she expected. In another, it is so on-the-nose that it feels like a message.

"Did you check for a familial relationship?" she asks.

"No. Not yet. I've only the Holloway family to draw from currently. Now, if I knew who these *other two people are...*"

Evie almost laughs. "Damn."

"Exactly. So I have to ask." He leans in, voice dropping. "Where did you get these hair samples?"

The Harbinger lands a blow to her chest, a hit that feels almost like panic. It is not a flavor she's accustomed to; most times the entity is cold, precise, disdainful of emotion. This is different. This is more a 'Shut your mouth. Say nothing.'

Evie looks at Liam, watches his jaw set, the slight tic at his left eyebrow. She decides.

"I took a detour through Oklahoma," she starts. "There was a field, an underpass... and some remains."

Liam's eyes narrow, sensing the gravity of her words.

"Remains? A Jane Doe?" he asks.

"Yes," Evie nods. "The hair, the build—it was eerily similar to your Missouri victim. It feels like more than just a coincidence."

Liam leaned in closer, absorbing every detail. "And what about the other?"

"Emily Janes. She's an Ohio victim from several months back." Evie continues, her voice softening. "The mortician knew her. Felt bad for the girl, and kept a lock of hair. I got him to open up and share it with me."

She shares no mention of Mercer, the black ops teams, or anything of the kind.

Liam's mouth is a hard line by the time she finishes. "No two ways about it. This is deliberate selection. Least, except for the Rayburn girl."

"Someone is building a set," says Evie. "Matching up donors with a recipient with specific needs, so specific it could only be done with high-level data."

Liam's shoulders rise, then settle. "Jesus," he says. "How much do you want to bet there's more?"

She nods. "It's a pipeline. You don't build something like this for just one run. They're harvesting, refining."

Liam is quiet for a long moment. When he speaks, it's as if he's balancing on a blade: "Did you share this with anyone else?"

"Not yet," she says. "Wanted to see how it hit the ground first."

Liam closes the folder, tapping it against his palm. "I'm going to take this to the team. State level, maybe higher. Work out the pattern."

He looks at her, a question on his face.

"Are you ready?" he says. "We could use the extra brainpower. Plus, seeing as how right you are about this, you might catch something the rest of us miss."

The Harbinger's chill spikes, a migraine nailed behind her eyes. 'No.' Its word is absolute, thunderous.

Evie keeps her composure. "I'll reach out to Haden's crew at Quantico," she says. "They have specialists who know the math. If anyone can see the meta-pattern, it'll be them."

Liam seems disappointed, but accepts it. "That's good. All hands on deck, then."

She nods, grateful he didn't press.

He stands, zipping his jacket, folder tucked under his arm. At the door, he pauses. "You sure you're okay?" he asks.

She is about to lie, but then: "No," she says. "But I'll get there."

He smiles, just enough to remind her that the world has not yet stopped making decent people.

"I'll keep you posted," he says.

He leaves, shutting the door gently behind him.

Evie sits at the table, staring at the manila folder, the rapid DNA printouts lined up like a triptych. She feels the Harbinger slinking back into its corner, sullen and stewing. The pressure in her skull ebbs, leaving only a faint residue of cold.

She knows what she has to do next, its a professional obligation to a job she no longer holds. She powers up her laptop, opens a blank email, and hovers over the keyboard. For a moment, she allows herself to believe that if she types the right words, if she deciphers the code...

Her fingers begin to freeze.

Chapter Twenty-One

Unheeded Warnings

The freeze starts at her fingertips and coils up her wrist. Evie shakes her hands, first in irritation, then in anger, as if she could exorcise the Harbinger's will by muscle memory. She slaps her palm down, breaking the chill, and pushes off from the table.

"You will not stop me," she says aloud, to the empty motel room and whatever is lurking just outside perception. The air vibrates with a faint whine, like old copper pipes knocking against a freeze.

Fine, let's escalate.

She snatches her phone, thumbs through her contacts until—Director Haden's number.

Evie turns. The mirror over the cheap dresser is alive with haze, the shape within not hers. Not quite. The thing gathers in its reflection, its skeletal-like form loose, as if assembling from half-remembered stories. She approaches the glass, jaw set.

"You're not going to stop me," she repeats, her voice steady, a profiler's monotone. "They need to be brought in."

Its face flattens to a rictus, all teeth and vacancy. Deep eye holes glare back, but with that distant, cold light—as innumerable dead compressed to tiny points.

Her thumb stabs the 'Call.' button. The dial tone launches into rings, but it's somewhat off: too slow, too deep, as if the frequencies warp a fraction toward an abyss.

With each ring, the thing in the mirror grows, outstripping her height, then filling the upper half of the frame. Its hands grip the frame and lever forward, distorting the glass as if it were thickening.

Four rings. The world loses focus. Her lungs won't fill, the air thinning to the texture of freezer burn.

Five. The mirror flexes, thin cracks spreading from the corners. The Harbinger's mouth opens wide enough for the jaw to dislocate, then wider, and wider still.

Six. The phone hisses and dies. The thing lunges.

Evie reels back, but the arms—the hands—are around her, every inch of skin not skin at all, but static, a thousand nerve endings assaulted in pin pricks. She tries to fight, but the force is both inside her and around her. The Harbinger's cold flows through her bones, up her spine, and into her head.

There is a moment when she is nowhere, and everywhere. And then she falls.

The stone is cold and flecked with red. Darius the Lesser crouches at his desk, stylus in hand, scratching lines of cuneiform into the wax tablets as fast as the words come. His beard is oiled, his hands elegant, but now both drip ink and sweat. The candles sputter. He presses on, knowing time is blood.

Above, thunder; below, the clamor of feet, as the garrison closes in. He writes in code—old Avestan, the tongue of the forbidden priests—but the message is simple: 'The king's men will betray the Empire, villagers blood spent, and if you are reading this, prepare to run.'

The door bursts open. Soldiers in lamellar scale, eyes blank as dolls. A satrap, his voice nasal and rich, sneers at the scribe, then signals with two fingers.

Darius drops the stylus and tries to kneel. He pleads with his eyes, but the iron grip on his jaw stifles his mouth. A dagger is unsheathed, curved and gleaming. The satrap does not shout, nor gloat, nor explain. Instead, he commands.

"Silence him."

The blade slashes. Darius feels the heat first, then the cold, as his tongue is severed and the inside of his mouth fills with copper. The world narrows. He falls onto the stone. His vision spots and swarms. Above him, the satrap signals again. The soldiers drag him from the room.

In the dusk courtyard, his wife and two children are herded toward a wall of fresh-cut limestone. Masons are already at work, mortar slathered, the first course of bricks rising fast. His wife sees him—her eyes wide, mouth open in a scream he cannot hear, not over the gurgling roar in his ruined throat. The children are small enough to believe it is a game; they hug her legs, their cheeks streaked with snot and sand.

They are forced to kneel. The masons begin to close the gap. Each brick seals another patch of sky, another axis of hope. Darius tries to rush them, tries to use his body as a wedge, but the guards hold him back, their faces blank, bored.

He watches as the wall climbs, his wife's face visible for a few bricks more, then just her hand, fingers reaching, then nothing. The air thickens with lime dust and the stink of fear. Darius is thrown to the ground and left to bleed.

His vision blurs. Chill permeates his body. Then...

In the woods, 1864, Tennessee. The trees are black against the moon, branches like old bones. Lettie Green crouches at the base of a walnut tree, her dress pulled tight around her legs. Her hands are wrapped in a man's scarf, but they shake anyway, more from hunger than cold.

Down the slope, a lantern bobs, the voices of men carrying over the brittle ground. She waits for them to pass, then counts to thirty and slips from her hiding spot. Her feet are bare and numb. She knows this ridge—has run it a hundred times, delivering coded messages between Union sympathizers in the valley. She knows which rocks are loose, which roots will twist your ankle.

At the far end of the ridge, Lettie finds the marker: a nail scratch on a granite boulder. She kneels, scrapes a shallow pit, and tucks the folded message inside, wrapped in a twist of blue cloth. As she stands, a branch cracks. She freezes.

A man in a gray coat is behind her, rifle at the ready. His eyes are red, sunken. He says nothing, but motions with the barrel. Lettie's heart pounds; she lifts her chin, refusing to give the note away with her gaze.

More soldiers appear, their uniforms tattered, faces shadowed by hats too large for them. One holds out a hand; she gives him the cloth. He unrolls it, sniffs, and then spits. The leader steps forward, black-gloved hand trembling as he draws a pistol.

They force Lettie to walk ahead, down to the valley clearing. Dawn is smearing the clouds red, and for a moment the world seems unreal, painted in blood. In the clearing are a dozen men, women, children—her kin and neighbors—lined up with their hands bound. Lettie sees her uncle, the pastor, mouth working in silent prayer. She sees her little cousin, boots two sizes too big, staring straight ahead.

The soldiers tie ropes to the branches, hanging the nooses with methodical care. Lettie stands at the front. A man reads her note aloud, laughing at the fancy script and big words. He tears it up and lets the pieces drift into the dirt.

One by one, they kick the stools. Their bodies jerk, then sag. The only sounds are the creak of rope and the wind in the grass. Lettie kneels, numb, as the last man—the black-gloved one—points the pistol at her face.

She closes her eyes. Lettie feels the gun's muzzle on her forehead. She does not beg.

There is a click. Then...

Berlin, 1938. The world is damp, smoke-strangled. In the basement, Erich Wendel huddles in his overcoat, the lining frayed, the pockets stuffed with notes and thin cigarettes. He listens at the vent, ears attuned to the words of the doctors above, his heart slamming against his ribs.

He has seen what is happening at the Institute: the sterilizations, the 'cures' worse than the disease, the body parts kept for research. His hands shake as he sorts the files—photographs, signatures, orders stamped in eagle-red. He knows he will not make it out alive, but someone must know.

Wendel's wife is expecting, her belly a small planet orbiting their shabby apartment. He promised her he would run, but he cannot—not until he has delivered the names to those who could act. He finishes the last page, slides it into the envelope, and creeps up the stairs.

At the door, two men in gray stand, backs to him, arguing over cigarettes. Wendel slips past into the freezing dawn and makes for the government office. Inside, he finds a clerk, a thin woman with nervous hands. He pleads. She shakes her head, eyes wide, and calls a number on the wall phone.

Wendel is led into a side room, the envelope confiscated. He is told to sit. For hours, no one comes. He bites his nails until the fingers bleed, then tears the cuff of his shirt for a handkerchief.

Eventually, two men enter, faces indistinct but voices low and smooth. They sit across from him, open the envelope, and read the names. One offers Wendel a cigarette. He takes it, his hands shaking so hard he can barely hold it.

"We thank you for your concern," one man says, in flawless German. "We will see that the matter is handled." The other one nods, then snaps his fingers. A third man appears, gloved and silent, and they lead Wendel away.

He is brought to an unmarked building, down stairs that echo with each step. The hallway is lit only by the flicker of bulbs; there are stains on the walls, some fresh. He is put in a room, hands cuffed behind his back, and told to wait.

On the table in front of him is a single photograph: his wife, boarding a train. He wants to weep, but there is nothing left. A man enters. He levels a pistol at Wendel's head.

Wendel looks up, wanting to ask if she is safe, if the child will be born. The man simply shakes his head.

There is a sound like a door slamming. Then...

Evie's eyes snap open. She is face down on the motel carpet. The phone is buzzing beside her, but her hand cannot grip it. She feels the pins-and-needles of returning sensation, pain mapping her nerves in hot, crisscrossed lines. Her breaths are shallow, ragged.

Propping herself up, she slumps against the bed. The mirror is blank—just a sheet of silver, reflecting only the smear of her own exhaustion.

She knows, with no need to reason it out, that the Harbinger has delivered its response: messengers don't last. Truth-tellers are punished, their lines and bloodlines snuffed and sealed away. Every time, every place, the result is the same. Betrayal, execution, erasure. Not even family survives.

The phone screen is black, unresponsive. She hurls it at the pillow and buries her head in her arms, willing the vision away, but every time she blinks, the images cycle again—blood on stone, nooses, a bullet in the skull.

Evie didn't just see... she witnessed it!

The trauma is hers now.

After a time, she stands. Her legs are rubber, but Evie forces herself upright. She pulls her jacket on, the cold nestles in the lining, and walks to the window. Outside, the parking lot is empty, the sky bloated in the midday light. She opens the window, just enough to feel the chill, to let the air nip at her face.

Her urge to warn Director Haden is gone. Not suppressed, not simply blocked—but carved out, as cleanly as a tongue from a mouth. She will not call. She will not send the message.

The Harbinger has ensured that.

The profiler part of her brain catalogues the lesson: the Harbinger's interest is never personal, only proportional. It cares nothing for motive, only for effect. The warning was not about the Bureau, not about Haden, not even about justice. It was about entropy, the way systems always seek to erase threats to their balance.

Mercer is a threat. Mercer is the one who's drawn the gaze of the ancient and the angry. Mercer, with his endless reach and money and men who will kill for a patch and a cause. Even thinking his name feels like lighting a match near dry kindling.

She has to keep this hunt alone. The message is simple. Share it, and you'll feed the wall, the rope, the pistol.

Evie shivers, then steadies herself at the sink. She wets a towel, runs it over her face, and winces at the tenderness in her shoulders, where the Harbinger gripped too tight.

Her phone, forgotten, chirps from the bed. The notification is soft, but it thrums. She steps over and taps the screen.

> **ETHOS: We've hit pay-dirt.**

She opens a new response, thumbs out the words:

> **EVIE: I'm here. What've you got?**

Before she hits send, she looks once more at her reflection. The room is still, the air thin, but she feels a new clarity, the cold flame of purpose burning behind her eyes.

She presses send.

Chapter Twenty-Two

Vanta Dark

The aftertaste of freezer burn still lingers on her tongue long after the Harbinger's grip has faded. The clock on the motel's microwave says it's been barely half an hour since Liam left. Evie sits on the edge of the bed, laptop open, cursor blinking.

The Ethos channel is alive, with a tide of usernames rising and falling in real time. CtrlZ, RootMuse, HeapMonk, and a dozen more, blink in and out as if the forum itself were hyperventilating. No video, just text; any face shown here is a needless risk not worth taking.

She enters. The welcome is instantaneous, and a little desperate.

CTRLZ: WAS STARTING TO WORRY YOU FLAMED OUT

EVIE: Here. Did you find a window in?

ROOTMUSE: We got a goddamn skylight

HEAPMONK: We are in, we are so far in I can see the other side

She keeps her replies brief. There are always more lurkers than visible hands, and even among the so-called white hats, the loyalty is more about mutual gain than any actual trust. But tonight, the urgency is different.

> CTRLZ: We're at phase three. Grid is heavy but not impossible. You see the access logs?

> EVIE: Skimming now

She scrolls through the logs. The pattern emerges: a brute-force assault on Mercer's server network, each hit logged and mirrored, but with a flavor of resilience that's both admirable and deeply messed up. Mercer appears to have an A.I., branded as Vanta, managing his vast online architecture. Of course, he does. Vanta is Mercer's pet, Mercer's weapon. It absorbs each of Ethos' attacks, quarantines the IP, and then, instead of counter-attacking, just logs the event and flags it for human review.

> HEAPMONK: This thing is not like anything I've ever seen.

> ROOTMUSE: It doesn't fight back. It just watches. Like it's learning from every hit.

> CTRLZ: We're stacking the logs now. Trying to choke the input but it's a black hole.

For a second, the oddity distracts Evie. Any normal defense system would lash out, start blacklisting whole net blocks, maybe even try to hack back. But this... thing is passive, almost curious. Each time it catches a probe, it responds with a digital handshake, like it's thanking the attacker for the lesson.

CTRLZ: Got a weird one here. Some of these blocks are—hold up

ROOTMUSE: Ctrl?

CTRLZ: They're not routing to the same end node. There's a secondary port, off the main grid, patched to a live cell.

HEAPMONK: You mean Vanta is phoning home?

CTRLZ: No, not home. It's pinging out to a cell number. Like, every time a critical access attempt is detected, it sends a snapshot of the attack to an encrypted burner. Then it goes dead for 10 seconds, like it's waiting for a return call.

ROOTMUSE: You think that's Mercer's line?

CTRLZ: No idea yet. But there's more than one number adjacent to this chain.

Evie sits up straighter, nerves taut. She ignores the lingering ache in her back, focusing in on the moment.

EVIE: Can you isolate the numbers? Any of them match known residences?

CTRLZ: Running it now.

The thread fractures as two of the secondary hackers—one who calls himself Gremlin, the other just D8—drop in with chatter about traffic spiking in odd intervals, always just after Vanta pings out. Like a clock signal for a much bigger operation.

> D8: Look at this. I've a phone here with hits to Cincinnati, St. Louis, and the middle of nowhere in Texas.

> EVIE: Wait. Is that Wichita Falls?

> D8: Good guess. Give that girl a root-shell.

Those locations... Cincinnati (Milford), St. Louis (Moscow Mills), and Wichita Falls... That's not Mercer! *That's my organ harvester!*

> CTRLZ: Hold on. We got a pattern.

The chat slows. The weight of a realization passes from user to user, all the way through to Evie, sitting in her motel room.

> CTRLZ: I'm clocking two numbers marked as priority. One, always in or near Geneva, Zurich, or New York. High finance triangle, classic Mercer. D8's one is mobile. Midwest, southbound, always for less than 72 hours. It's on the move now. Currently in Kansas City.

> ROOTMUSE: If it's Mercer, he can't be in two places at once.

> EVIE: It's not Mercer. It's his cutout.

> CTRLZ: Your killer?

EVIE: His killer.

HEAPMONK: What?! You're saying Vanta the A.I. is feeding him? Like, live?

EVIE: Could be. If he's just a delivery vector, not an originator.

ROOTMUSE: So, Vanta is picking victims.

CTRLZ: Or vetting them. Running them against some recipient database.

EVIE: Makes sense. All three matches had compatible genetic markers. That's the only reason you'd cross so much data so fast. How much current info do you have on that number?

CTRLZ: Checking. The phone is in KC, pings a hospital, then a steakhouse, then an address registered to an Airbnb.

HEAPMONK: You got the address?

CTRLZ: [Redacted for the forum, but a private ping to EVIE: 1617 Cypress. Suite C. 2nd floor. Host is a physician, private practice. Check-in was 7:45 PM. yesterday.]

ROOTMUSE: How long until the next delivery?

EVIE: If it's like the others, no way to be sure. But his window is short.

CTRLZ: You going to call the cops?

She types nothing for a while, hands knotted on the tabletop. The Harbinger's warning still pulses in her mind, a second heartbeat, but her own need for closure is louder.

EVIE: I'm going.

CTRLZ: Solo?

EVIE: Yes.

ROOTMUSE: That's messed up.

EVIE: If I wait, he'll have another victim. At the same time, I sure as hell can't share how you gained me illegal access to the cellular database.

The forum falls silent. Then HeapMonk, in a rare moment of vulnerability:

HEAPMONK: Good point.

CTRLZ: If you need backup, ping us live. We'll be watching.

EVIE: Copy that.

Chapter Twenty-Three

It's on Her Now

The air in her motel room is different, charged with something ferrous, as if the Harbinger's visions had salted the walls. Evie stands by the window, curtain drawn just enough for a shard of winter to edge in. She watches nothing, listens to less.

The forum cursor on her laptop still blinks. She closes it, folding the device with reverence. It's always been her weapon of choice—a profiler's scalpel, capable of mapping the rot out of any pattern, any man. Yet when she wraps the power cord around it, her hands shake, just a flicker. There's an impulse to smash the computer against the cinderblock wall, but instead, she tucks it into her battered go-bag and moves on.

She has lived a good chunk of her adult life around her organized home base, not in motels: one chair, two lamps, a bedspread meant to resist both stains and sentiment. She packs quickly, stripping her presence from the space in order of reverse importance: laptop, notes,

DNA reports, the disposable camera from Oklahoma, even the yellow stick of gas station jerky. None of it slows her.

Evie wipes the mirror with her sleeve—an urge, maybe, to blur any trace of what had emerged from it.

The Harbinger's presence hasn't left. It's less a voice, more of a cold viscosity in her joints. She wants to shake it loose, but that hasn't worked yet. Instead, she inventories her own state: fatigue at the eyes, adrenal shudder in the neck. Evie clasps her rosary, cycles her breathing. She is alive. But not quite in the way she was yesterday.

Tossing her bag on the bed, she sits, letting her weight settle the mattress. The lines of memory align: The mortician, Moscow Mills, Laney's hair from Wichita Falls, the ditch in Oklahoma. And always, the pattern of the victims—matched, refined, recursive. With Mercer's unseen hand guiding the process, Vanta feeding the targets, and then the Deliverer, some Slavic ghost moving through the world in surgical increments.

She is alone, but not at all.

Her solitude feels like every new layer written over the old. She thinks of Haden, the only man in Quantico who ever believed she had a mind worth weaponizing. He used to say, "The people who can see the worst in others rarely see what it does to themselves." He said it after her first big bust, the one where she'd nailed the killer's signature down to a single blue Bic pen and the serial number on an invoice. She was 26, full of contempt and caffeine, and already knew she'd never sleep easy again.

After Haden came the rest of them: Marcus Vaughn, who wore his ego like a Kevlar vest and still blamed her for every case he couldn't close. Cassandra, the analyst who could keep pace with her, but had quietly distanced after the Cross family breakdown. Reyes, still a cop's cop, but never quite trusted Evie's statistical angle over a gut hunch.

She'd burned them all in different ways, sometimes with words, sometimes by holding her silence.

But that's what happens when you think in meta-patterns: people become nodes, and every connection is another opportunity to corrupt the chain.

The thought makes her heart pitch. She bends forward, elbows on her knees, and rests her head in her hands. It's not tears—she's not built for that anymore. It's more of a dull ache, a pressure in her orbital sockets that feels like duty and regret all at once.

The phone on the nightstand vibrates, a wasp boxed in plastic. She ignores it. Then reaches for it anyway, thumb hovering above the lock screen. The message lands with a thud.

> LIAM: Any word?

It's only been about an hour since he left. But then things were moving at a clipped pace.

She stares at the words for a long time. Her thumb glides above the letters, never connecting. She wants to answer him honestly. Evie wants to tell him about the danger, the entity in the mirror, the way the dead speak to her in the language of nerve endings and trauma. She wants to type: I'm scared, but not for myself.

Instead, she puts the phone down, screen still bright.

She packs the rest of her belongings with mechanical precision. The scarf—a gift from her daughter, purple, soft, too small for an adult but she keeps it, anyway. She packs her toothbrush, then the little travel bottle of whiskey she keeps for nights when sleep is an adversary.

Evie stands and circles the room one last time, looking for anything left behind. Her shadow moves with her, but there's an echo in it—a lag, as if her body has outpaced its own reflection. She thinks of the Harbinger, its lesson: messengers do not survive. The image of the tongue being cut, the wall being bricked, the gun at the base of the skull. It is a warning, but it is also a comfort. The choice is hers.

She grabs her bag, keys, and opens the door. The sidewalk is empty. She walks to the car, boots clacking on the concrete.

Outside, the cold is absolute. She likes it. The way it shocks the breath, the way it makes every nerve stand at attention. She unlocks the Fiesta, throws her bag in the back, and slides into the driver's seat. Evie pulls the door shut and sits, letting the silence fill her.

The phone buzzes again, twice, then three times. It's Liam, persistent as ever.

> LIAM: You're probably tied up in Fed speak.

> LIAM: Don't let jurisdiction be a roadblock. MO is currently open door.

> LIAM: If you need me to follow, I can be wheels-up in 20.

Evie grips the phone hard. She wants to type: I'm not worth the chase. Or: Stay safe, because I can't guarantee anything. Or even just: Thank you.

Instead...

> EVIE: All good. Will update once things pan out.

She hits send and immediately regrets it. The message is a dead thing, with no warmth, no context. It's the kind of message you send to someone you don't intend to see again.

Evie puts the car in gear, pulls out of the parking spot, and merges onto the empty highway. The afternoon sun is out now, but it does little to stave off the cold. She checks her mirrors, nothing but blacktop and the shrinking outline of the motel.

As she drives away, there is a physical sensation—a slow uncoiling at the base of her skull, a clarity she hasn't felt in months. The decision has been made; the mission is hers alone. There is freedom in it, bitter but real.

She glances in the rearview one last time, the phone screen visible in the cup holder. She hopes Liam will understand someday. Maybe when it's all over, maybe when they meet again, or not at all.

Evie mouths a silent apology, then grips the wheel tighter.

The road is empty, but she knows better. She is never alone. Not really.

She drives on, the presence beside her neither friend nor enemy, but a force as old and inevitable as hunger.

It is enough. For now.

Chapter Twenty-Four

Hunting Grounds

The drive into Kansas City is a slow-tightening garrote hidden in the local traffic. The skyline is neither impressive nor shy; it's the kind of city that keeps its business in warehouses and its crimes in the infinite expanse of detached neighborhoods. Evie drives with both hands, forearms locked, letting the Fiesta's tires hum their intent across the cold concrete.

At some point, her inner chill transitions from a presence to a purpose. It doesn't fight, it just sits behind her eyes, soaking in every detail as if noting the memory for later. The highway signs thin. She wants to keep her own mind clean of static, but the phone blips on the dash—Bluetooth logo pulsing.

It's not a normal number. The caller ID is +44, followed by a random scatter of digits. Evie taps the answer on the steering wheel.

"Yes?," she says, voice flat.

The car's speakers fuzz, then: "Profiler. CtrlZ. Root is here too."

From the background, a second voice, cool and synthetic: "We are tracking the target. You are within three miles."

Evie's shoulder's droop a smidge. "How did you get my number?"

"VoIP endpoint. Your device handshake is public," CtrlZ says, as if it's obvious. "You want the update or not?"

"I'm listening."

"There's a ping from your killer's phone," CtrlZ continues, "a minute ago. It's a burner, but whoever set it up wasn't too worried about their paperwork. Probably fake. Bosnian passport, scanned and uploaded to the shop. Name reads Alexei Volkov."

Evie files it away, sharp as a pin. "Physical location?"

"He's piggybacking on the cell tower at North Congress Avenue. North side, big-box strip, half a dozen public Wi-Fi vectors. Our guess is he's on foot."

RootMuse cuts in. "We ran the phone against leaked app data—location brokers, delivery services, the whole shadow market. He's not using the device for calls, just for passives. You follow?"

Evie nods, though they can't see it. "So, what, it's a lure? A way to check if he's being followed?"

"In a roundabout way, yeah," CtrlZ says. "But the phone was active near a place called, Kansas City Cannabis Co. That's where the Wi-Fi handshake hit last."

Evie considers. She lets the car idle through a green light while she checks the online map. "There's a bar next to that. Arthur's Karaoke Lounge. If he's hunting for his next donor, it'll be there."

RootMuse chimes, "You have a plan?"

"Yeah," Evie says, and pulls off at the next exit. "Ping the phone again. Quiet, no alert. I want to know if he's still inside."

A pause. "Ten seconds."

She slides the Fiesta onto the access road, heart spiking as she passes a digital billboard for payday loans. The block is a mess of vape shops, fast-food, pawn, and then the Cannabis storefront, glass doors banded in green. The parking lot is mostly empty, but several cars are clustered near the karaoke bar: a Ford pickup, one matte-black Tesla, and a mix of Civics, Toyotas, and Chevys.

CtrlZ is back. "Ping returned. He's still connected to the public network inside the Cannabis shop. We see the device. But there's a second endpoint. You want it?"

"Give it," she says.

"Same make, different IMEI. It's inside the bar. Connected to the Wi-Fi, but the MAC address matches a vendor square terminal. Could be nothing."

Evie asks, "Root, you said the passport scan was lazy?"

"Sloppy. Some discount clerk just made a quick swipe of it. But a sub-vendor runs the software that handled the KYC. All their files leak, eventually."

"Send me the face," Evie says.

There's a digital hiccup, then a photo drops into her texts: a blurry shot of a man in his late thirties, jaw like a fist, pale eyes, close-cut hair.

"Copy," Evie says, then, "Stay close."

She pulls the Fiesta up to the curb, a half block from the karaoke bar. The sky is a pretense of blue; it's a color that means nothing in November. She kills the engine and sits, checking her phone once, then twice.

Evie debates the gun—her holstered Glock. She doesn't need a visible outline inside a bar, too much of an invitation. So instead, Evie stows it under the driver's seat, and tugs her jacket tight. She wants to be light, fast, nothing to catch a hand or a stare.

The karaoke lounge is bigger than the pictures suggest. Neon script writhes above the door, a melting "Arthur's" that promises two-for-one well drinks and no cover before seven. There's a bouncer built like a nightmare, hands already pawing through a college girl's Michael Kors knockoff.

Evie waits at the edge of the lot, watching the street. Two men in camo jackets share a cigarette by the weed shop's door; neither has the predator's posture, but she notes them anyway. She walks up the sidewalk, adjusting her stride for nonchalance.

The bouncer tracks her. He gives the girl's purse a desultory pat, hands it back, and then fixes Evie with the look of a man who thinks he's seen everything.

She waits for him to speak first.

"You here for the contest?" he says.

"Just scouting," Evie answers. "You running a bag check?"

His eyes flick to her pockets, her waist, then back up. "You'd be surprised what people carry in. Bongs, needles, once had a chick bring in a chinchilla."

Evie gives the man a thin smile. "Not my speed."

He shrugs, then extends a meaty hand. "Purse or jacket?"

She opens the jacket, lets him see there's nothing to care about. He waves her past.

Inside, the noise is a living thing. There's the pulse of country pop, the stutter of a karaoke MC making bad jokes, and the lingering fog of vape-smoke and fryer oil. The lighting is an insult to every shade of human skin, and the tables are crowded with the pretense of happiness.

Evie stands just inside, scanning for the face from the photo. Finding nothing on her first sweep, she moves to the bar and orders a club soda. Something within her spools around her core; a chilled thrum resonates. This must be the place.

Now, just wait.

Wait... and watch.

Chapter Twenty-Five

Third Wheel

Why is it always karaoke bars, Alexei thinks? America's truly democratic forum for the mediocre. Even here, in the booth's burgundy-shadowed corner, with a half-bottle of Svedka sweating between them, his donor can't resist watching the stage. Every time a shrill cheer goes up, Samantha's body tenses, small hopeful flinches, as if she's waiting to be called for judgment.

He wears her attention the way he'd wear a wristwatch—lightly, for utility, never for pride. She is younger than he prefers, but her blood chemistry and organ set are impeccable, and in this business, that is the only metric worth knowing. He nods, smiles on cue, pushes a lock of her hair behind her ear. She laughs as if it's a shared joke, oblivious that his touch is diagnostic: scalp density, absence of hairline trauma, pulse strong in the carotid.

At the next table, a pack of men in fleece vests raise a shot-glass salute to the TV's scrolling lyrics. The woman bartender—fat, ponytail—leans over to flick at the sound system. The entire room is a hyperbaric chamber of off-key anthems and suburban hormones. He resents the sticky optimism of it all.

Samantha—'call me Sam'—is on her third vodka-soda, and the giggle in her voice is splintering. "I can't believe you remembered my drink," she says. "Most of the dudes I date think vodka is just for frat parties. I mentioned, you have a face like you'd be a whiskey guy. Or maybe absinthe? Is that even legal?"

He lets his smile broaden, showing all the teeth. "Absinthe is over-rated. All the ritual, no payoff." He leans in, lets his tone slip to a hush. "You seem like someone who prefers results."

The blush that creeps into her cheeks is textbook. She is exactly the sort of person he once would have hated: born pretty, quick to mock, always chasing that next thrill. But she's the best match he's seen in three cities, and her tissue profile is worth more than the combined salaries of everyone in this place.

"I think we're going to have a lot of fun tonight, Alex," Sam says. "Unless you're just here to stare at me and say nothing." She punctuates this with a clink of glasses. Her nails are painted the same poison green as her purse.

"I'm not the staring type," he says. "I'm more of a... participant observer."

She seems to like this. Sam likely sees him as an interesting one, a little dangerous but safe in public. He wonders, as he always does, how this might read on a forensic timeline: the girl's last night, the drink, the disarming laughter, the scrubbed profile from a date she found online. That was a specialty of his recruiters taught him, erasing any trail.

He taps the edge of her glass. "Drink up," he says, "or the karaoke host will think you're too scared to sing."

Sam wrinkles her nose. "No way. I'm not getting up there. I picked this place only because you said you liked live music."

"This?," he says, and she laughs again, the sound pitched up with nerves. He wants her to finish the drink, but she's slow, savoring. He is patient—he always is—but tonight the clock is running hot. This batch needs to ship in less than 48 hours. If he misses his window, the price plummets.

He's about to nudge her when a lithe figure glides into the booth.

The new arrival is a woman—small, black, the sort of beauty that triggers more insecurities in other women than it does lust in men. Her eyes are large, framed by a mass of hair gathered in tight twists. She wears a gray jacket, jeans so dark they nearly vanish, and shoes that look neither cheap nor expensive, just clean. She slides in next to him, pinning him in place.

Sam sits back, already on defense. "Uh—excuse me? This booth's taken."

The stranger ignores Sam, turning directly to him. "What are you going by tonight?" she says so quietly it barely escapes the music. "Tell me it isn't something as unimaginative as Alex."

For the first time in months, his spine tightens. He keeps his face even, lets the half-smile linger. "Sorry, but you have the wrong guy."

She leans in, and for a moment, her hand rests on his thigh. It's a practiced gesture, calculated to seem intimate, but her fingers press hard enough to test his muscle underneath. "You're not supposed to be here," she says, "but you couldn't help yourself. They make it too easy."

He shrugs. "I get that a lot."

Sam glares, seemingly unsure if this is a joke or a nightmare. "Is this, like, your girlfriend? Because you could have told me. I'm not into drama."

The black woman doesn't even glance her way. Instead, she slides her hand up his leg, then with a magician's flair, extracts his phone from his pocket. He didn't even feel it. Impressive. She holds the phone away from him; the screen asking for a pin over his wheat field wallpaper.

"Nice," she says. "Something from the motherland?"

Alexei stares. He should be more alarmed, but his curiosity is outpacing his fear. Whoever she is, she's good. He glances around the bar, scanning for backup, but sees none.

The air between them crackles with threat and implications. Her voice is just above a whisper. "I know what you are," she says. "And who you answer to. But I'm afraid it's not going to go down the way you expect tonight."

Sam scowls, teetering on the brink. "Seriously, who the hell are you? This isn't funny. Alex, tell her to leave."

He holds up a soothing hand. "It's okay, Sam. She's just... confused."

But Sam isn't buying it. Her cheeks brighten with anger and embarrassment. "Whatever. You're both psychos." She slides out of the booth, finishing her drink in one furious gulp. Alexei watches her walk away. She doesn't look back.

He fires a ferocious gaze at the woman. "Now you've lost me a lot of money."

She shrugs. "You'll get over it."

He wants to grab the phone from her, but she's balanced perfectly in the booth, blocking his exit. He could easily pummel her, but thinks twice of that in an American country bar. That wouldn't go over well with the locals. Her smile is slight, almost bored, but her eyes are calculating every twitch in his muscles.

"You don't know me," he says.

"Al-ex-ei," she says, drawing out the syllables. "You're smarter than you look. But not by much."

He shifts in the booth, weighing his odds. Maybe she's one of his benefactor's people or possibly even a competitor. He wonders if this is some bluff, or just blackmail for a cut.

"Stop me when I land on the right one; FBI, FSB, GRU?" he says. "Interpol? You're not some—how you say—bounty trapper?"

She leans back, relaxing into the seat. "I'm a messenger," she says. "And you are going to listen."

His eyebrow cocks up. "Is this the part where you warn me off, or try some trade for information?"

She considers. "Neither. I came for your attention, no bargaining. Just wanted to see the sort who sell their soul for points on a spreadsheet."

He grins, cold and clinical. "You think I'm ashamed? My work saves lives... at least important ones."

"Whose, then? Mercer's? The men who pay to keep his arteries clean?"

"Who?" He shrugs. "You're projecting." He studies her face, trying to place the accent. It's American, but layered with something else—a precision, maybe military, maybe analytic. Her eyes are steady; her affect calm. There's a rage somewhere under it, but she has it under tight control.

He matches her gaze. "You know what they do in the orphanages where I'm from? In the hospitals with no medicine? Would have let me rot, or get shot for some political stunt. Instead, I'm the best. You know, they could use my data at places like your Johns Hopkins, Harvard, Mayo. Imagine the possibilities. Are you that sort of thinker?"

A beat of silence.

Alexei expects her to insult him, but she says: "You're right. I'm not."

He lets his eyes fall to her hands. They're small, her nails trimmed back to nothing. No jewelry, no paint, nothing to catch or hold. He wonders if she's carrying a tracker, or maybe just a recorder. It doesn't matter. He won't be around long enough for it to matter.

She leans in again. "I know you're planning to move on after tonight. Another city, another target? I also know you're expecting to walk out with a suitcase full of cash. But you won't."

He lets himself smirk. "And how will you stop me? I can still go for #2 on my list."

She rests an elbow on the table. "You'll be surprised."

He watches her. He could break her wrist in four seconds, maybe less. But this doesn't feel right. He's missing something. "You're not a cop," he says.

"Not anymore."

They sit in silence, the noise of the bar receding into a dull roar. He wonders what her angle is. Maybe she's nuts. Maybe she needs a transplant, and this is some elaborate American negotiation. Or maybe she's just bored and wants to see firsthand what kind of monster he truly is.

He finds himself oddly impressed.

Alexei decides to test her. "You know, you could have just sent an email," he says. "This is a lot of effort for a threat you can't back up."

She studies him, then asks: "What do you see when you look at me?"

He considers. "A girl who probably weaseled out of a straightjacket. Someone who believes she's immune to the rules. Maybe you are, in this country. But not everywhere."

She nods. "What if I told you I already know the outcome? That there's little you can do tonight that will change it?"

He chuckles. "You're a fortune teller now?"

"No," she says. "Just very good at reading the pattern."

He reaches into his jacket, pulls out his wallet, and lays a hundred-dollar bill on the table. "This is America. I'm sure we can make a deal."

She slides it back. "Really?"

He tries another tack. "I tell you what. I don't think I can salvage that one anymore." He glances over his shoulder; Sam is already chatting with a new group at the bar. "What if I allow you in to watch my next best candidate?"

Her mouth twitches, not quite a smile. "You have a sense of humor, I'll give you that."

He leans in, lowering his voice. "Let's cut the games then. If you're going to try to kill me, do it already. If you want to turn me in, good luck. I'm not fearful of women who hang out in karaoke bars."

She shrugs. "You should be."

He likes her, in a way. She's the only person in months to talk to him straight, with no pretense. He wonders whether she'd make a good partner. He doubts she'd ever let herself get close.

"I'm curious," he says. "Why me? There are worse men out there. Real butchers, not surgeons. What makes me so special?"

She looks at him, and for the first time, he sees a flicker of genuine anger. "You think you're a surgeon? You're a parasite. But you don't even know it. I thought maybe if I could see you up close, there might be a trace of remorse. Or even something... human."

He shrugs. "Well. Maybe next time then."

She stands, and for the first time, he feels the chill. Not in the air, but in the way she looks at him. Like she's sizing him for a coffin. She then pockets his cell phone in her jacket.

No, that's as far as she goes. Now, she has crossed a line. This girl cannot be allowed to leave with his phone, but more than that, Alexei wants her dead. He cracks his knuckles as he rises to tower over her.

At first, she doesn't look up. Still unafraid.

But then...

Head tilting back, her black curls reveal an unearthly stare.

He's never seen pupils like this. Not dilated, not even animal. Just obsidian and infinite, pulling all the light in the room into her skull. For one cold heartbeat, he can't look away. Ice rises in his blood, the way he felt the last time someone tried to kill him. This is the same: pure, clean, and indifferent. Her hatred—it's machine-grade.

Then death slides up over his shoulders, a snaking chill that pulls at the hairs on his skin. This is what she was holding back. *This is why.*

Chapter Twenty-Six

That which Follows

For a moment, Alexei thinks he is still in control. The next... the world unscrews from its hinges.

The chilled misty thing rising behind him looms over. Ethereal vapor blots the booth, ceiling, and half the bar, the shape both clear and impossible. Its eyes are infinite empty sockets, its mouth a slashed gaping maw. For a split second, he knows. He recognizes it, for every Slavic mother warns her children what happens when you let мёртвый (the dead one) in.

It's you he will come for.

Alexei glances wildly around. No one else sees it. Not the bouncer, not Sam now laughing amongst others at the jukebox, not the three wasted men at the next booth. They're completely oblivious!

Launching backward, he knocks the table clean off its post, bottles and glasses shattering into a wet snowstorm of glass. The dead one keels up over him. Its fingers are just wrong—too many, and too long.

He doesn't think; Alexei moves.

The bartender is yelling, already coming around her bar. The karaoke MC stares, mouth frozen on the first note of "Islands in the Stream." Alexei seizes the nearest weapon—someone's coat, a laminated menu, a water pitcher—and hurls it at the entity. They pass through. Of course they do. Of course!

The dead one laughs, but not with a voice. More of a vibration through the teeth. Each time it opens its mouth, the room grows colder. Alexei's joints stiffen, fingertips going numb. He's seen rigor, but never felt it marching up his own arms.

That black woman—the tiny one with tar pools for eyes—just watches. She doesn't move, doesn't even flinch as Alexei tears loose and barrels into the nearest patron, a fat man in flannel who absorbs the shock and crashes to the linoleum with a howl.

Someone tries to grab his arm. He whips around, throws an elbow into the man's face. It's a clean strike; he feels the bridge of the nose go soft under his forearm. Blood sprays onto the bartender's shirt. She screams, drops the towel, tries to backpedal but trips over her own feet.

Alexei leaps the bar, lands hard, kicks two bottles off the rail as he grabs a full liter of vodka in each hand.

The dead one is waiting on the other side. It's not even trying to be quick—it just looms overhead, a glacier in the shape of death.

He throws the bottles at it. They pass through, and explode against the spinning fans overhead. Shards of liquor and glass rain down on the patrons.

Snatching the bartender by the wrist, Alexei uses her as a shield as he pivots, angles for the far door. "OUT!" he screams at her, not for her sake but so the others clear the path. She breaks from his grip, sprinting for the fire exit. He follows, but the crowd converges, the bouncer having recovered and now charging from the lobby side.

That black-eyed woman, silent and methodical, walks behind the dead one, her movements unhurried.

Alexei tries to run, but his legs are bricks. He swerves, grabs a chair, and uses it to bulldoze three bystanders. One goes down hard; another bounces off the padded arm and lands on the karaoke stage. The dead one lunges closer, its face melting and reforming into a thousand variants of his mother's, his instructors, every woman he ever failed.

He babbles in Russian. "Сука... сука... сука..." It doesn't help. His native tongue won't save him in this place.

Alexei pivots, slams the bar stool into the bouncer's shin. The crack is beautiful; the man's howl even better. His next beat is a punch through the clot of civilians by the exit, his left arm windmilling. Someone claws at his jacket, rips a button free, but he is already gone.

He explodes out the door, into the parking lot.

The cold night air is a relief. He's out. Alexei lurches for his pickup truck. Fumbling for his keys, he drops them. "Чёрт!" He slams a palm against his thigh, digging for focus. The dead one emerges through the bar doors, its face now less human, more animal.

Flinging the truck door open, he throws himself inside. The seatbelt sticks; he ignores it. Engine coughs, stalls, then catches. Alexei guns it to reverse out of the space, wheels spitting gravel.

In the mirror, the dead one is a smear of gossamer white; the black-eyed woman appears behind it—hands at her sides, chin down, still watching. The darkness of her eyes widens as he slams the transmission into 'drive.'

He is shaking so badly he nearly veers into a Prius as he barrels out of the lot and onto the street.

For a split second, he wonders if this is a psychotic break, a trick. But the aches from his scuffles, the blood on his pants, the way the cold is still burning his lungs—all confirm: this is not just insanity.

He floors the pedal, praying to every dark god in the Slavic pantheon that the thing behind him doesn't know how to drive.

He hits the first light at nearly 100 kph, barely making the turn onto the feeder ramp. The city blurs by, a palette of streetlamps, all of it hostile. He checks the rearview: nothing but the afterglow of rage and fear.

But he knows it is not over.

He bangs his fist against the steering wheel, cursing out, "Чёрт, Чёрт, Чёрт." Alexei breathes in and forces his brain to be rational. If it is a stalker, a mimic, a projection—it doesn't matter. There's always a limit. You should have a plan.

Plan. Yes. There is a plan.

If ever compromised, if the FSB or local police or anyone with a badge gets too close, he is to break off, cut all contacts, and run with the fallback. Nothing fancy—no kill box, just pure bureaucratic judo. Turn yourself in, but as the wrong person. Give the Americans a problem, and they're only too eager to solve.

He needs distance.

The next few minutes are pure noise. He whips through the I-29's sparse traffic, weaving in and out of lanes. Warehouses, hotels, then the unlit sprawl of shipping facilities with no reason to be open after dusk. He risks a glance in the mirror.

There are headlights back there which are not just keeping pace; they're gaining on him, low and boxy. The vehicle passes under the lights; it's some crappy Ford car, the color of tarnished nickel. He laughs, a thin, hysterical noise. Even now, she's still there.

Alexei knows the dead one is not in the car behind. He frantically scans all the surrounding spaces. It can be in the gaps between the cars, in the shadow of the on-ramp, at the moment when you're alone and you know the next second is your last.

His foot leans harder on the pedal.

Ahead, the illuminated flat box of a terminal and the tower of the Kansas City International Airport approach rapidly. He flies past the short-term parking, weaving up the ramp and skidding his F-150 to a lurching stop outside the departure loading zone. Alexei kills the engine, hurls himself through the lobby entry, and into the warm lights of the lobby.

He wipes his nose with his wrist, fumbles for the passport in his jacket. Bosnian. Only a year old, but a quality forgery. Now, he just needs to leave it to the good old U.S. Immigration. They'll take him away and deport him to Sarajevo, not Moscow. And from there, he can vanish for real. That's what he tells himself, but mostly he just hopes it'll get him away from that thing.

Focus. Next steps.

Security is a roped corral of sweating, overdressed people, each one a potential obstacle. He pushes forward; the line parts just enough for him to force his way through. Those he leaves in his wake glare in affront. He threads the labyrinth, cutting under belted stanchions until he reaches the battered blue ones at the front.

"Sir, you need to—" says the first agent, but Alexei just pushes in, slapping his passport on the TSA agent's podium. His words tumble out, not just nervously but at gale force, his Slavic accent tuned to the frequency of urgency.

"I am Alexei Volkov. Am illegal. Entered from Canada, no visa. Surrender. I want to surrender."

The TSA woman's jaw goes slack. There's a second of absolute confusion before she barks, "Supervisor here, now. Get ICE. *Now.*"

Alexei keeps both hands flat on the table, fingers splayed wide so nobody shoots him. He struggles to arrest his breathing. He's made it. He's safe. They hustle him down a side corridor, one hand on his elbow, the other scanning the perimeter. He glances back one last time, hoping she's gone.

On the far side of TSA, she is standing there.

Nothing in her hands, nothing on her face. Her hair is a little wild, her coat zipped all the way up. But it's her eyes. No whites, like obsidian marbles, unblinking. Before security shoves him through a side door, he sees the black-eyed woman turn... and walk back outside the terminal.

His lips twist into a grin; it's so perfectly unfair.

TSA seat him in a small room, hands cuffed, but not tight. They leave him for a few minutes. He hears their phone calls, probably to ICE. There will be files to process, fingerprints to run. He sits back in the chair, letting the relief drain through him like a spinal tap.

He'll get his American right to a phone call. Notify his benefactors he's triggered the fallback plan, and that chíka won't be able to do a damn thing to stop him. "Heh..."

Yet, there's a vacant thought floating in his mind. A blank space itching at him—the number. He didn't memorize it. It's in his...

He pats his empty pant pocket.

"Чёрт!"

Alexei lets slip a nervous laugh, the sound small in this quiet room.

Chapter Twenty-Seven

Noose Slipped

Outside the terminal, the air tastes different—like the hollow between two storms, charged and raw. The Harbinger's exit from her body draws at her senses like a pulled tooth. For a moment, she stands, unable to register how she got from the bar to the airport sidewalk; the next, she's taking notice of her Fiesta idling in the marked drop-off zone.

It's a full minute before her awareness resolves: she's upright, coat zipped high, standing three feet from a concrete pillar. Her teeth ache from clenching. The chill is back, but it's just the Midwestern winter settling in.

Now what?

She has nothing. No badge. No warrant. No evidence that proves Alexei is her killer. The Harbinger's anger, for once, is a comfort; somehow it is made easier sharing this entity's frustration.

Evie's pockets are unbalanced, too heavy on one side. She fumbles a hand through and finds—yes! The phone. Alexei's phone. She must have pocketed it before the world went fuzzy. She turns it over in her palm, studying the battered case, the micro-abrasions on the screen.

Above the rumble of cabs and idling SUVs, she hears the faintest echo: not a sound, but a resonance, the aftershock of the Harbinger's angst. It wants more. It wants—what? Closure. Justice. Or maybe just to see someone pay in a way that sticks.

She can relate.

A tap on her shoulder. This airport security guard is tall, early twenties, face trying for stern but defaulting to uncertain.

"Miss? You can't park here," he says, words diffident but practiced. "If you're waiting for someone, there's a cell phone standing zone just around the loop."

"I know." She pockets the cell, raising her hands. "I'll move."

He tips forward. "Do you need help? You look..." He squints, searching for the right word.

Evie nods. "Cold."

Drawing a breath, he rights himself. "Yeah, it's brutal out." He tugs at his safety vest as if it could warm him. "Terminal police are handling a situation inside, so it might be a bit before things clear up."

"Okay. Thank you," she says, and starts walking.

It isn't until she's ten steps away that she realizes: The police are dealing with Alexei. More than likely, the TSA will keep him in custody for at least an hour. After that, ICE will take the handoff to wherever is next in the food chain. She's seen the system work enough times to know: they'll run his prints. If there's no hit on NCIC and he doesn't contest deportation, then, in a day or two, he'll be expedited onto a flight to Sarajevo or wherever that passport promises. Once there, Mercer's machine might scoop him up, launder his identity, and drop him into another hunting ground. And the pipeline—the pattern—continues.

She has a day. Maybe less.

The only thing she has in her favor is the phone.

Evie gets in her Fiesta and slams the door, welcoming the silence. She digs out her own phone—battery at 18%—and texts CtrlZ.

> EVIE: Model: Oppo K9 patched. Four digit PIN. No biometrics.

Three seconds later, the reply:

> CTRLZ: Wait. You get him?

> EVIE: No. Slipped the noose. But I have his cell.

> CTRLZ: Got it. U ready for unlock?

She doesn't answer. Instead, she starts the car and checks the rearview. Nothing but halogen lights and the security truck guy waiting for her to move on. Evie puts it in gear and eases forward toward the airport exit.

After passing only two blocks, she pulls into a shipping/receiving company. Its parking lot is nearly deserted after hours. This will provide her with the quiet space she needs to work.

Letting the engine keep her warm, she boots up the ThinkPad, balancing it on her lap, and opens a chat window. CtrlZ is already waiting, the cursor bouncing in an impatient staccato.

> EVIE: Ready.

> CTRLZ: Did he power it off before handoff?

EVIE: No. Pulled live.

CTRLZ: Good. Here's the exploit—

A code block appears, with instructions so concise they make her nostalgic for her own time as an analyst. She follows each step: disables mobile data, enables ADB via the laptop, and runs the payload. Within a minute, the phone unlocks, the home screen reveals a wallpaper of a snowy pine forest, possibly Russian or maybe just generic stock.

EVIE: We're in.

CTRLZ: You want me to pull an image, or you driving solo?

EVIE: Solo for now. Will ping if I get stuck.

CTRLZ: Be careful. These guys run tracking on their own devices, sometimes bomb code.

She reads that last line twice. It isn't paranoia if it's true. Doubt ICE will give Alexei access to a phone for a while still. Mercer's people are currently in the dark, but no way of knowing for how long.

Evie scrolls through the apps. There are a few American ones here: Bumble, Tinder, Grindr, and Instabang. Also, two encrypted messengers (both in Cyrillic), a fitness app, and a folder marked TOOLS with six utilities, all side-loaded and unsigned. The call log is clean. The SMS folder is empty. But what get's Evie's attention is the Airbnb app.

After scrubbing through his password manager, Evie comes up with the app's pin. Easy enough. And like that, she's in. This profile is for a Jason Carter, from Pittsburgh. The rental is roughly five miles from here. Makes sense. He's sticking close to an airport, for a fast out just like he used.

Next, Evie scrolls through the Cyrillic messenger. No phone number associated with the other party, simply an encrypted user profile of random letters and numbers. That seems like something the Vanta A.I. would do. And copying/pasting Cyrillic from a cell phone to a laptop is not something easily accomplished in her Fiesta. It'll wait.

For now, Evie needs to see what he's got at home.

She screenshots the rental entry and messages it to CtrlZ.

> EVIE: Found where he's staying. Going to check out.

> CTRLZ: You're playing with fire, profiler. Amazed you're not burned yet.

> EVIE: Copy that.

> CTRLZ: You ok?

For a moment, she doesn't know how to answer. The chill in her arms, the brain fog, the way her hands still want to shake—they're not side effects. They're the cost. But for once, she feels a flicker of optimism. He's not gone yet.

> EVIE: Tip top.

Checking the other folders, there's a Note app. It holds a series of what look like codes—hexadecimal, likely onetime pads or VPN keys. She copies them out, sending to CtrlZ with a single caption: "Triage."

Finally, in the Tools folder, she finds an app with a red icon, nothing in English. She launches it, and a login prompt appears. The password autofills, and a dashboard emerges: three columns, each with an icon and a timestamp.

The first column is labeled "Подобрать," and the most recent entry is tonight's date, with a confirmation mark. The second column, "Транспорт," lists two cities:

Moscow Mills and KCMO. The third, "Поставки," is blank, except for one line: Z6, Суббота 22:00, and a red warning triangle.

She screenshots everything to him. CtrlZ doesn't reply right away, but that's normal; he's already feeding it into Ethos' composite.

With nothing else to do, she switches over to her own phone, and checks her messages.

There's one from Liam, time-stamped twenty minutes ago.

LIAM: Any news from the Feds?

Damn.

Chapter Twenty-Eight

A Glimpse Within

She's had bad ideas before, but this one requires precautions; like wearing gloves. The Airbnb is a stucco townhouse in a planned community where all the lawns share the same stubble and the curbs never stain. The key box code is right there in the app.

Inside, it's a living room with taupe walls, a couch that's never known a real nap, and the sort of wire-sculpture décor that only ever looks good in a listing. She closes the door and listens: nothing. No footfalls overhead, no TV from a neighbor.

Evie texts CtrlZ;

EVIE: In. Will ping if I need anything.

CtrlZ: Log everything

She snaps photos as she walks—doorknobs, electrical outlets, the faint indentation of a suitcase roller in the hallway carpet. There's a slight chemical smell, not bleach, not exactly. Maybe a composite cleaner or one of those "air-purifying" candles you see at high-end spas. She clocks it, moves on.

Kitchen first. There are three foam coolers stacked by the fridge, and beside that a heavy-duty device the size of a mid-size office Xerox. Its white hard shell has a digital readout and is bracketed by two sturdy handles. This hefty machine means business. She opts to lift the lid on one of the lighter foam ones: inside, a triple layer of sealed gel packs, a vacuum bag, and below that, nothing. It's not loaded yet. But it is intended to be. This is not improvisation; it's protocol.

Under the kitchen table: four bottles of hospital-grade surface sanitizer, three boxes of nitrile gloves, and a pack of industrial lint-free towels. There is no food in the fridge, just a bottle of off-brand energy drink and two bottles of Gatorade, blue.

The master bedroom is unremarkable. She checks the closet—sliding doors, a single winter coat, and tucked in the back, a clear tote bin labeled "SUPPLIES." Inside: three sizes of plastic sheeting, two rolls of duct tape, a hardware-store staple gun, and a portable LED light array with a snap-on battery pack. She flicks the light on; it's blinding, casting shadows that stutter and double. Having had enough of that, she clicks it off and tucks it back.

The bathroom is generic, except for a small black carry-on on the floor. That she opens, expecting clothes, but it's all medical: surgical scissors, suture kits, scalpels still in shrink, arterial clamps, and a little vacuum-sealed envelope of blue surgical gowns. Everything is labeled in English, with manufacturer stamps that say "For Research Use Only."

At the bottom, she finds a pouch with a USB stick and a folded piece of paper, torn from a legal pad and written in blocky ballpoint.

She flips open the note:

Z6 - HEART (PRIORITY)

- S. LANDERS ($150k)
- E. STONE ($95k)
- J. MENDOZA ($89k)
- C. SANTOS ($81k)

Each name has a dollar value penciled next to it, but only the first $150k is circled.

She reads it three times, the names thumping like a pulse in her head. The killer's donor list, his entire market logic, right here in borrowed English.

Evie checks the bathroom mirror. There is nothing there, just her own reflection, eyes a little bloodshot, skin dull in the light. She waits for the Harbinger's presence, the dry-ice bloom of its intention, but it's quiet. If it's here, it's watching in silence.

She sits on the edge of the tub and tries to connect the dots. The victims are not random; each is a match, a top pick on the harvest list. The only anomaly remaining is the delivery mechanism. Once Alexei has his product... how does he confirm for delivery?

She needs to know. It's the only way she's going to follow the chain back to its source.

Evie boots up her ThinkPad, plugs in the USB. CtrlZ's exploit runs in the background, mapping out the files. There's only one folder: "Vanta Drop." It's full of charts, tissue matches, health metrics, even psych profiles. Mercer's A.I., Vanta, had refined the list to a science. For each target, there's an address, last known, and predicted movements.

But no mention of the drop protocol. No way to know how the organ changes hands, only its qualifications.

Scrolling through the files, she clicks faster, growing more and more frustrated. What is she missing? An ethereal sense creeps at the base of her skull—less a threat, more an insistent nudge. It wants something now.

She stands in the dead center of the living room, still holding the phone. The air is dry. Yet, the answers do not present themselves. What more does it take?

Let go.

Evie clicks off the room lights, and for a span, allows the pattern to run.

At first, there is nothing. Then, like a low wave—a chill blooms at her collarbones, filling her lungs. She opens her eyes. The room is no longer empty.

In the sliding glass door, a shape waits. Not reflected. Not real. But it's there all the same: a figure, limbs indistinct, a face composed of negative space, the suggestion of bone, a smile wide and understanding. It does not move.

She stares at it. Unafraid, but every cell in her body braces.

"What," she says, not even aware she's spoken. "What do you want?"

The thing in the glass lifts what passes for a hand. It points to her, then to the kitchen, then to the phone. Then, it simply waits, its form haloed by the night outside.

Evie follows the gesture. She checks the phone. No new messages.

In the kitchen, the gel pack sweats beads from its open lid, but otherwise, nothing.

She examines the phone again. *Yes.* The Cyrillic messenger, of course. But what's the code they use?

Grabbing her laptop, she connects Alexei's phone via a USB cord. Evie breathes in, holds it, then walks to the couch, sits, and pulls up her Ethos chat. CtrlZ is standing by.

> EVIE: Our mark's phone is mounted and jail broken. There's a messenger system in Cyrillic. Go to town. Show me what we've got.

> CTRLZ: Game on.

She glances up. The thing in the window has not moved. It merely waits.

Moments tick by. Then, a scrolling thread of text rolls out in a fresh window. The translation was simple, but what they got back... not so much.

> ALEXEI: branches are filling in nicely

> SKEX!21: Make sure the fence is sturdy | Water only at night

> WOBS$84: By the light of the silvery moon

> ALEXEI: basket is full

The messaging chain goes on and on. Each day's phrasing shifts from gardening to pottery to knitting, etc. Each reply is a random username—most likely Vanta code-switching. *Damn.* Only Alexei will know what's next.

From the darkness, the Harbinger is close—closer than it's ever been. It's not a voice, not a feeling, but a compulsion, a directionality: if you want to know what comes next, you must complete the pattern.

Reflected in the sliding door glass, her face is half-shadowed, but behind her, the Harbinger hovers—now part of her outline, fused at the spine, the shoulders, the hollow behind the ear. Its eyes—not eyes; its mouth, a wound.

She doesn't flinch.

Instead, she stares it down, and lets the coldness overtake her.

The supplies are in the kitchen. The phone. A sense of intent climbs up her spine. Evie is not going to get the answers. It is not up to her to do that now. But they will come, all the same.

"I understand," she says. "Collect what's needed."

The Harbinger does not reply. Its mouth widens, filled with a rictus meaning.

Evie stays like that, mirrored and unmirrored, until the cold is just another part of her. She blinks, and the reflection is gone.

She knows what she must do.

It's going to be a hell of a haul, but she needs that machine. Evie ignores the foam coolers and pulls on the big device. It weighs almost as much as she does! That just won't do. She'll need some gear. Guess adding a dolly will be one of them. Grabbing up the tote, she dumps the rest of the medical supplies into the bag. Evie finds a black windbreaker in the closet, throws it on over her jacket. Loading what she can into her car, she moves with the steady rhythm of someone who has already accepted the outcome.

But she knows what she has to do.

Evie leaves, not bothering to lock the door. She won't be long in coming back for the rest. The air outside is sharper now, the night deeper. In the parking lot, the wind cuts through her jacket, but she barely feels it.

The world is simple in this moment: there is a task, a target, a delivery. Much like this Deliverer, the one within her will do the thing no one else can.

Chapter Twenty-Nine

Wait Too Long

The thing about conference calls is that they're like death by slow hypothermia: you barely notice you're freezing to death until it's hours too far gone. Liam Hayes has spent his day in the thick of it—State, County, and even City suits all pitching their wisdom across a bullet-pointed minefield, everyone wary of taking an actual step. By the time he's allowed to extricate himself, the world is already dark, the parking lot's frost glinting under street lights.

His drive home is uneventful, a minor miracle. The Missouri River is out there in the dark, flowing beneath the bridge in total disregard for the human entropy at its banks. He pulls into his drive, parks the truck, and turns off the ignition. In the weak dome light, he stares at the dashboard. What if he restarted the engine, backed up and just drove, maybe to the next county, maybe all the way out to the badlands past Columbia? But he's not a man for that sort of drama.

Never has been.

The radio cuts out with a last gasp of Merle Haggard when he opens the cab door. The house is quiet and cool, but that's how he likes it. He walks in, not bothering with the lights, and toes his boots off at the mat. There's a dish in the sink—a glass from last night, the crusted rim of lime and salt marking the last time he felt halfway human. He ignores it and heads for the den.

The laptop is lid down but not fully asleep. He cracks a beer from the garage fridge, sits, and logs on. Not even ten hours since he last checked his inbox, and there's a new flurry: St. Louis, two from the state Attorney General's office, all variations on the same update. Progress stalled. Investigation still processing. No new victims, but nothing moving on priors either. The professional jargon is worse than a ransom note. He closes the laptop.

He checks his phone. No missed calls, no messages from Evie. He told her to keep him posted. He almost texts again, but the screen lights up with his own last message—"let me know if you need me"—and the white void beneath.

Don't get all needy now.

Liam nurses the beer for a while, letting the silence do its work. Eventually, the cop in him digs: why hasn't she replied? Why haven't the feds swooped in? Everyone knows that's what they're known for. Something doesn't fit. It's starting to feel like it never has, but now the edge is sharper.

Opening the laptop again, Liam is more determined. He doesn't search for the case. He searches for her: Special Agent Evelyn Cross.

It's easier than it should be. The old press hits are there: Child Prodigy Joins Bureau, Whiz-Kid Cracks Midwestern Serial. But then, five years ago, the rupture. Daughter of Michael and Evelyn Cross abducted. The body was not recovered, presumed dead.

My God.

Liam scrolls through the coverage, piecing it together. There's a quoted photo—Evie at a podium, eyes red but dry, voice described as "unflinching." The comments are the usual mix of sympathy and venom: How can an agent lose her own child? How can she keep working after that? Liam feels something catch at the back of his throat. He's known a lot of tough men and women. He's known no one who lost a child and kept breathing, let alone stayed on the job.

He clicks through to the next story. It's an anniversary piece, three years after June's abduction. The reporter tries to spin hope, but it's mostly just grief pornography, more stabs at the mystery of how an agent could not recover her own flesh and blood. Buried in the middle, a throwaway: "Cross has not given interviews since the Bureau pivoted her away from the Cartographer case."

Liam sits back, absorbing it. The analyst in him wants to distill it into a bullet: Cross's daughter abducted, never found, Cross keeps working, but something broke inside her and never healed.

The beer is warm now. He dumps it, gets another, and paces the kitchen. If it were his own kid—if he had a son all those years ago, had been snatched—he'd have burned the world down to get him back. Would have moved heaven, just torn up the blacktop with his own hands to reach hell, if need be. He'd never have stopped. And that's what's bugging him: Evie hasn't stopped either, but she's doing it differently. She's running silent, playing by rules he can't see.

All the cases, all the patterns she tracks—it's a proxy for her own loss.

He checks the time. It's almost ten. He will not get a reply tonight. But the thought won't die in his head: what if she's found something? What if Evie has gone after their suspect alone, to finish what the system couldn't?

Flipping through his contacts, he dials the FBI's Quantico number. It rings seven times before the switchboard picks up. Detective Liam Hayes identifies himself, says it's important, and the bored-sounding operator says she can transfer him to the Supervisory Agent's voicemail. "He's out for the night, sir. Unless it's urgent."

What if he's wrong? *Jump to conclusions much?* Not exactly an ideal way to connect with a pretty lady.

"No." Liam relents. "Not urgent. Go ahead and put me through."

At the sound of the tone: "Agent Haden, this is Detective Hayes, of the Missouri State Patrol. I've been working a local case with your Agent Cross lending a hand. But haven't been able to reach her for most of today. Please call back, even after hours. This is an unofficial—but official matter." He hangs up, suddenly aware of the sweat under his arms.

If only he could ping her phone. He's done it before, with a proper warrant, but he knows damn well the FBI is locked down tighter than a vault when it comes to their own. Without a favor from Haden, he won't get authorization.

He spends the next twenty minutes scrolling through the news, the online obituaries, even the Reddit boards devoted to unsolved crimes. No mention of Evie. No new posts about organ traffickers. Nothing about missing law enforcement. The world is static, holding its breath.

Liam thinks about texting her again, but erases it. Instead, he just types: "Hey. Thinking of you. Let me know you're safe." He doesn't send it.

He stands in the kitchen, beer in hand, feeling the weight of other people's losses stacking up like cordwood. Liam isn't much of a praying man, but he does promise, in the silent, cold grammar of his mind, that if she needs him, he'll answer. That's what a man should do. He'll answer.

The phone doesn't ring, not even once.

He sits at the window, lights off, watching the frost creep up the pane. The world beyond is full of things that can never be fixed, only observed. He thinks of the river, the way it keeps moving even after you stop looking. He thinks of this poor woman, her daughter, the hollow in her voice when she spoke of hope. It all makes sense now. Her wounded persona. Lost hope because it was already too late.

He'll wait for Haden's call. He'll wait all night if need be.

It's what he can do.

Chapter Thirty

The Lounge

Getting deported from the United States is, on balance, less humiliating than the recruitment interviews at Russian medical school. No one laughs at your accent, for one. No one spits in your hair, or asks if your mother worked in a whorehouse during the recession. Even the ICE officer who processes him wears gloves and addresses him as "Doctor Volkov." The honorific tickles.

Alexei has spent the past twenty-four hours at the Chase County Detention Center. It is in his estimation superior to at least half the hospitals he rotated through in St. Petersburg. His sheets are polyester, true, but clean. The air conditioning doesn't rattle. Their food is an abomination, but so is American cuisine generally, and here at least, there is the pleasure of knowing that your calories are measured and the salt content is sufficient to keep you pickled against mold. The only part he finds wanting is the security: his "cell" is more of a reinforced dormitory, and he has to share it with an Armenian whose only crime, apparently, was overstaying a student visa and posting unkind memes about the Turkish embassy. They bond over a mutual contempt for U.S. television, but otherwise keep to their own corners of the bunk.

It is remarkable how quickly the system bends to make him someone else's problem.

He watches now, elbows on his knees, as the ICE officer—barely older than the Armenian—rifles through a ream of paperwork and double-checks a digital screen. Her name is Parsons, though she has yet to volunteer it to Alexei. She is compact, with brown hair cropped into a bureaucratic helmet, with a faint suggestion of a birthmark along her jaw that she camouflages with foundation. If she recognizes him as anything but a routine Tuesday, she is either a consummate professional or has seen so many war criminals that he simply does not register.

He likes her for this.

She completes her review, closes the folder with a judicial whack, and looks at him over the barrier glass. "It's your lucky day," she says. "Expedited order. Chicago tonight, then off to Belgrade."

Alexei feigns concern, tilts his head. "Just a layover, yes?"

"Don't worry. They're not letting you off the leash until you're back in the homeland. You'll have a couple of hours at O'Hare," she says, her voice flat. "But you're not leaving the secured lounge. My supervisor will meet us there for the handover."

Lounge? Nice.

He holds her gaze a fraction longer than necessary, then drops his eyes in deference. "You Americans," he says, "always so efficient."

She doesn't reply, but her lips flicker in a suggestion of a smile. She rises, steps around the glass, and gestures for him to follow. He does.

They traverse the underbelly of the detention center: the world of steel doors, camera globes, and hallways washed in hospital-grade lighting. It is cool here, and the only sound is the click of her boots and the heavier, more deliberate step of the second ICE officer who flanks him. He is tall, broad at the chest, with the face of someone who expects you to respect him automatically. He never addresses Alexei directly, which is a shame; the man would be so easy to antagonize, one could probably get him to swing a punch within ten words. But Parsons seems to have expected this and walks just fast enough to keep the threat unfulfilled.

In the sallyport, she hands over his plastic-wrapped belongings: the jeans and windbreaker, the off-brand running shoes, the battered wallet, his counterfeit Bosnian passport, and, best of all, his favorite pen. He left the good wristwatch at the airport, knowing they'd just confiscate it, and he is curious to see whether the TSA at O'Hare will show the same discipline when he's inevitably processed through their meat grinder. But for now, he has his pen.

She let him change in a small cubicle, with the Armenian lounging on the opposite bench. Alexei takes his time, inspects the shirt for stains, and admires again the craftsmanship of the passport. It is, he must admit, one of the best money ever purchased. Not even a hint of raised laminate, no weird chemical smell. He checks the photo: it is a perfect lie, almost bland in its earnestness, the kind of face you would see in an Eastern European driving school and immediately forget.

It is almost a shame, he thinks, to torch it after use. But such is life.

He sits on the bench, turning his attention to the television in the holding tank. CNN, as always, is running a segment on the "border crisis," this week's panic starring a family of Guatemalans and a scowling talking head who seems incapable of blinking. Alexei wonders idly how many times a day the newscaster is forced to read the words "illicit human trafficking" without a trace of irony. He finds it almost erotic, the doublethink of it all.

He is so engrossed that he almost misses Parsons' return.

"Let's go," she says, and there is a new tension in her posture—not quite fatigue, not quite caution, but the aftertaste of some bureaucratic drama that has reached her by phone while she was away. Her eyes flick to the Armenian, then back to Alexei. "You're on your own from here," she tells the other man. "Mr. Volkov gets a special chaperone."

Alexei cannot help but smile. He mouths a silent "good luck" to the Armenian, who shrugs, noncommittal. They do not shake hands.

The exit to the detention center is not a grand portal, but a nondescript steel door. They pause long enough to gently apply steel handcuffs. Formality, really. Then the door is swung open. It is nearly sunset; the world outside is rendered in alternating stripes of pink and gray. The air has the bite of approaching winter, dry and sharp, and Alexei is reminded briefly of childhood train stations, the taste of copper on the wind, the way the snow would crust atop the benches so you had to brush it away with your sleeve.

At the curb, a white government van waits with its hazard lights ticking. Parsons opens the side door, and gestures for him to climb in. The second officer, silent as a rock, sits in the front passenger seat. The van's interior is spartan—no cages, just two cloth seats and a black steel plate between the front and back. He wonders for a moment if this is a test. If he tries for the door when they stop at a light, what happens? Does Parsons shoot him? Does she chase him, get a raise? Or does she simply sigh and mark it down as a learning experience for the next time?

She buckles him in. He crosses his legs, waiting for her to drive.

The sun is low as they merge onto the highway, and the trip to the airport is uneventful. The officer in the front spends the first ten minutes scrolling on his phone, then eventually succumbs to a brief nap, head bobbing against the glass. Parsons drives with the calculated boredom of someone who has done this route a thousand times, her hands at ten and two, her face in profile always slightly unreadable.

Alexei breaks the silence. "I do not suppose there is food at the airport?"

She doesn't look at him. "You'll get something on the flight. Unless you want a protein bar."

He considers. "Thank you, but no. I dislike chewing anything synthetic."

She snorts. "You'll love Bosnia, then."

This is the first hint of humor he's seen in her, and it pleases him. "Are you coming all the way with me?"

"To Chicago. Then you're another agent's problem."

"A shame," he says, and lets the compliment dangle.

They drive another 15 kilometers in silence, the van now swimming through the growing gloom of suburban sprawl. At some point, the city's edge falls away, and they pass the sign for the international terminal. She pulls the van into a cordoned loading zone, flashes her badge to the bored rent-a-cop, and parks next to a cluster of SUVs. The airport is bustling in the way only American airports can be, every inch of the curb packed with SUVs and minivans and swarms of people wheeling gigantic, half-empty suitcases.

Parsons opens his door and waits for him to follow. "You know the drill?" she asks.

"I have flown before, yes," he says. "Just not as cargo."

She gives him a look that is either pity or vague appreciation, then nudges him toward the entry.

Inside, the light is even brighter. The hum of the HVAC, the endless echo of the announcements, the bleat of security tones. Alexei is processed through a secondary checkpoint—less invasive than the police but more annoying, because they insist on removing his shoes even though he is clearly under escort. He wonders if Parsons will make him hold her hand, like a toddler, but she does not. She simply keeps pace, always one step ahead, never looking back.

Once through, a uniformed airport staffer leads them to a small glass cubicle labeled "Transit Detainee Lounge." The cubicle is barely large enough for the two of them, and an ancient iron rack attaches the chairs to the floor. Parsons sits, opens her folder, and begins filling out the departure paperwork. Alexei folds his hands in his lap and scans the TV bolted above the door. This time it's sports.

He waits until she finishes signing, then says, "Do you get to choose who you escort, or is it random?"

Parsons tucks the folder away. "You're not special, if that's what you're asking."

"I would not flatter myself," he says. "But you seem... less irritated by this than your partner."

She shrugs. "He thinks you're mafia."

Alexei studies her. "And you?"

She sets her jaw as if bracing for an argument, but then sighs. "I think everyone is a crook if you push them far enough. Some are just better at paperwork."

He laughs at that—real, deep, and for a moment almost honest. "Very true."

She glances at her phone, then at the clock above the TV. "Boarding is in forty minutes. You need the bathroom, go now."

He takes her up on it, because it is true: the first rule of transit is to empty yourself before you're stuck in a chair for the next two hours. She stands outside the restroom, arms crossed, not bothering to follow him in.

Inside the stall, he takes stock of his body. No new bruises. No sign of death shadowing him, at least not in here. But the dreams last night were exceptional—he woke twice, sweat pouring from his spine, the phantom pressure of those cold hands stretching for him. He wonders, not for the first time, if this thing will follow him across the Atlantic, or if it is an American haunting, like opioid addiction and reality television. He suspects it will wait, bide its time, see if he's foolish enough to return to the States.

Alexei is not.

He flushes, washes up, and returns to the 'lounge.'

Chapter Thirty-One

The Dead One

It starts with the illusion of order: fluorescent light, the clock above the television moving in disciplined ticks. Parsons has her paperwork ready before the official even comes for them. The escort is a TSA floater with little to prove—young, bored, nearly transparent in his utility. He asks Alexei to stand, applies a light touch to the upper arm, and walks them out of the 'lounge' into the artery of the terminal.

The cuffs remain on, but discreetly. Parsons drapes her black windbreaker over to cover them. "Don't need to make a scene," she says, not unkindly. The air is an inviting blend—brewed coffee, with just a trace of burnt popcorn from a cart up the concourse. It feels like one of their malls.

The gate is a ten-minute walk. Alexei moves quickly, almost enjoying the clear path provided by a badged escort.

"We're boarding you last," Parsons says, not quite making eye contact. "Plane is already loaded. No window for you. Turns out I was wrong. No food on this leg. Too short a hop to Chicago."

Alexei keeps pace, counting security cameras and noting blind angles out of habit. There is nothing to escape to really, but he still prefers to know the weak points.

The terminal is a latticework of people—fat businessmen half-unbuttoned from their day, a nervous cluster of teens in church trip t-shirts, a retiree with a dog. It's the world's least likely threat environment, but he feels the eyes, the unseen ones, floating around the corners.

They reach the last branch, a glass corridor with a view of the blacktop and the blinking wands of ground crew. Parsons slows, glances at her phone, and gestures for them to pause at a vending machine.

"Thirsty?" she asks.

He considers. "Yes."

"Pick."

He nods toward the water. She buys two, hands him one with the cap loosened. He takes a sip, letting the cold soak his teeth.

"You okay?" she asks.

Alexei blinks, surprised by the question. "Should I not be?"

She snorts. "Most people about to get black-bagged don't act so... calm."

He shrugs. "My country is full of bad endings. I am not a tourist to this."

She likes his reply, or at least registers it. For the first time since the intake, she seems a touch less brisk. Parsons drinks her own water, wipes her mouth with the back of her hand, and checks the time.

The glass corridor is empty. They walk. Thick carpet deadens the sound of their footfalls, but the air vibrates with the pressure of everything Alexei is not saying. He follows her lead, eyes forward, but the side panels of glass invite the mind to wander.

Halfway down, he sees her.

Not Parsons, not the bored escort. Reflected in the outside darkness, parallel to their movement, is a woman: small, black, hair up in tight spirals, coat zipped to the chin. She paces them, matching every stride. Her eyes are empty, marbled obsidian, unreflective. She does not move her head, but he feels the stare burn through the corridor.

He flinches, but doesn't slow.

At the far end, the reflection breaks; the woman is gone. The world returns to normal, if only on its surface.

Parsons senses the change. "What?" she says, not stopping.

Alexei says nothing, but she pulls him aside, out of the footpath.

"You see something?" she says.

He debates. "You will think I am crazy."

She smiles, a flicker. "You and everyone else here."

He gestures back. "There was a woman. In the glass."

She follows his finger, sees nothing. "There are a lot of people at the airport, Volkov."

He shakes his head. "Not like this."

She watches him. "You want to talk; now's the time."

He almost does. The urge is there, clawing behind his sternum: I am being haunted, followed, cursed by something I do not believe in. But he says instead, "Can we just go?"

She gives a tiny nod. "Yeah. Let's get this over with."

They walk the last stretch to the gate. Two staffers behind the desk, both on phones, neither interested in the passing of a man in cuffs. No other passengers. Parsons hands over the boarding papers, gets a nod, and they're waved to the jetway.

Then it happens.

Parsons pauses at the threshold, hand bracing against the bulkhead. "You okay?" Alexei asks, voice almost breaking.

She squints, unfocused. "Just a head rush—"

Her words garble. She reaches to her nose, touches it, and comes away with red. Not a trickle; a bloom. For a moment, she doesn't register the meaning. Then her knees buckle. She drops to one side.

The other guard is slow to react. "Ma'am? You—" He stops, looking from her to Alexei, then to the sudden, inexplicable pool of blood that's collecting on the carpet.

Alexei's cuffs fall open.

No one touched the locks. The mechanism simply gives out, both bands clattering through the windbreaker, to the carpet in a sequence so clean it could have been staged for television.

The lights overhead flicker, just once. Then again, longer, casting the corridor into a seizure-bright strobe. In the alternating slices of dark and light, the air seems to move, as if displaced by a rush of invisible hands.

Alexei recoils. He backs against the plexiglass, eyes scanning for the source.

There. On the ceiling. Crawling, liquid, moving in the negative spaces between the flashes: the Dead One. It's a shape of congealed shadow, joints bending at the wrong angles, face a mask of absence, and in its jawless mouth, the unending rows of teeth, all grinning.

He shouts. Not words, just a raw, animal cry.

The guard goes for his radio, fumbles it, drops it. He's fixated on Parsons, who is now spasming, her arms out, unconscious. In the strobe, she looks like a marionette yanked by strings.

The Dead One drops, lands in a heap next to her, then straightens, joints popping audibly. It looks at Alexei, only Alexei. Its hands—eight fingers per side, each digit a length of dripping bone—reach out.

Alexei runs.

He sprints past the writhing form of Parsons, past the gate crew. The Dead One launches after, not fast, but inexorable, unbound by friction or inertia. It flows more than chases, moving just under the fluorescence as if feeding on the light.

Alexei takes a blind turn and finds himself back at the concourse, now empty except for the echoes of his own footfalls. The ghosts are there. All their starry-eyed faces: the girl from Cincinnati, the guy from Moscow Mills, the Oklahoman woman. They cluster in the hall, hands outstretched, starlight pouring from their wounds, forming a gauntlet he cannot pass.

He slams a fist into the window, fracturing the glass, but it doesn't yield. The only way forward is through them.

He does.

Their hands claw at him, cold and unreal, but they don't slow him. They just fill his ears with a chorus of voices, whispering in every language he's ever learned: Thief. Butcher. Parasite.

He bursts onto the next jetway, the Dead One riding his shadow, nearly on him.

A red exit sign glows at the far end. He punches through the crash bar, and stumbles out onto the tarmac.

Night air sears his lungs. The ground vibrates with the churn of engines. To the left, a 737 idles, turbines spinning. The roar is absolute. He runs, dodges a baggage trolley, nearly slips on a patch of de-icer.

Glancing back, the Dead One is behind him, giving chase but not close. It moves in stutters, appearing and reappearing at impossible angles, always advancing, never pausing.

He angles toward the service road, but the ghosts are there, too. They fill the space, hands raised, voices now unified in a shriek that overtakes the engines.

Desperate, Alexei darts past the fuselage of the jet. Air sucks at his jacket, yanking him back. Its intense vacuum nearly rips him off his feet. The Dead One looms toward him, riding the airflow, jaws wide as it closes in.

In that moment, the cockpit window opens. A pilot, hair slicked back and face unreadable, leans out and sees Alexei. Their eyes lock for a split second.

The pilot slaps a switch. Engines spool down, turbine whine dropping. The suction relents. The Dead One's trajectory shifts as it ricochets up the fuselage, skidding along the slick paint, before being thrown clear into the night.

Alexei collapses, scraping his knees on the asphalt. He rolls over, and half clambers up onto a luggage trolley. His hands are tingling, his vision pulsing with afterimages. He waits for the icy grip on his shoulder, but it doesn't come.

Instead, he hears shouts—real people, panicked. Two ground crew members rush toward him, one with a walkie, the other with a stack of orange cones. No, he can't let them catch—He looks for a weapon. Anything! From the trolley, he brandishes a pry bar.

He staggers to his feet, swinging the pry bar like a madman. The two crewmen pause, then begin to backpedal. Just offside of the gate, the Dead One hovers on the edge of the lights, waiting, glaring. Not done.

Neither is he.

Alexei bolts away from the terminal, away from the runway, toward a distant promise of a hangar. Behind him, his ghosts scatter, then reform, hanging in his periphery. The Dead One keeps pace, never too far, but not closing the gap.

He knows it will be with him now, forever.

Yet he runs anyway, every cell in his body screaming in terror and a single, overriding need: to not die the way he lived. Alexei must find something... someway to fight it off.

He sprints into the darkness.

Chapter Thirty-Two

Flight of the Deliverer

The tarmac drops away, replaced by crushed gravel, then grassy earth—just the wind and the ragged shape of his breath. Alexei keeps the pry bar tight in his right hand, his shoulder throbbing with every pump. The airfield is a patchwork of colorful lights and shadow, but the far perimeter is true black. He angles for a low ridge beyond the auxiliary runway, head down, shoes slapping up ice shards with every footfall.

His body wants to quit. The lungs, never robust, start to lurch; his knees, once well-trained, now wobble like a marionette's. It's the adrenaline, the fear. Too much. There's a moment where his vision closes in, the world tunneling toward a single black vanishing point. For a second, he almost gives in—almost, but not quite.

At the far edge, a chain-link fence bows out from years of wind. Alexei drops his shoulder, running into it, just to bounce back. Trailing along the links, he spots the opening and lopes onward through it.

The hangar looms ahead, half a football field of pale cement with its main rolling door slivered open just enough for him to squeeze through. The Dead One is nowhere in sight, but he knows better. Alexei cuts a tight zigzag, checking every blind corner, and slaps the side wall before ducking in.

Inside the hangar is quiet. Not even the click or whir of a cooling engine, just a mute vacuum where all sound should go to die. He pushes the rolling door closed behind him, inch by inch, eyes always fixed on the margins. When he's satisfied, he stands, chest heaving, letting the pry bar dangle like a promise from his fist.

Nothing. No movement. No cold spike at the base of his skull. But he can feel it, the same way you can sense a thunderstorm through an old bone.

The space is mostly empty, save for a metal table in the center, bare except for two empty tool trays. Three mechanics' caddies line the east wall—snap-lidded, low to the ground, more for oil and rags than for weapons. He checks them anyway. The first: nothing but socket sets, a dead flashlight, three broken bits. The second: more rags, soaked through with dirt and petroleum.

Alexei keeps moving. The third caddy is locked. He kneels, pops the hasp with the pry bar, and finds—a set of small pliers. He pockets the pliers. Anything is better than nothing.

Still no sound, no movement. But the air inside is growing colder.

He scans for exits. The only other way out is a service door in the far corner, lit by a faint green glow of an exit sign. No windows, no roof access, nothing but blank walls and a stretch of painted concrete.

The service door is fine with him. The cavernous hush swallows the scuff of his steps. Halfway there, he slows, every nerve on alert for the taste of ozone or the scent of old earth. But it's only the cold.

At the door, he hesitates. The exit sign flickers, then steadies. He presses his ear to the steel, listening. Nothing.

He pushes the handle. It sticks, but he leans his weight, and it pops open with a muted sigh.

On the other side, standing framed in pale light, is the girl—the woman—his stalker, but not as she was. Her hair is a shining twist of curls; her skin is leached of color. But it's the eyes that kill the world: solid, uniform black with two infinitesimal pinpricks of ice-blue buried deep in each. She stands perfect still. Her hands relaxed at her sides. There are no weapons in them, only the certainty of a predator's patience.

He nearly slams the door in her face. Instead, she speaks.

"This is far enough," she says. Her voice is wrong: reverberant, all the emphasis on the wrong syllables, as if a synthetic chorus is parsing human emotion.

He recoils, backs two steps, feels the hangar's air thin. "Stay back," he says, voice ragged from running. "Whatever you are, stay back."

She advances a step, the movement so smooth it looks like a cut-and-paste on a bad video feed. "You escaped us once. Consider us impressed. That will not happen again. We are here now. All of us."

He glances left, then right—nowhere to go. He rears with the pry bar, but she just looks at it, then back at him.

"Though you have no way out, it's not entirely too late," she says. "Give me an answer. How do you make the exchange?"

He tries to step around her, considering the question a distraction, but she mirrors every movement, always there in the door's threshold. He could grab something else from the table, maybe use the metal trays as a shield, but deep within he knows the odds are bad.

"Who are you?" he says, stalling. "What are you?"

She tilts her head, the motion a slow and deliberate parody of confusion. "You know. You know what you have done. We are the only thing that remains... that remembers."

He thinks about making a run, but something in his chest tightens—a dire cold, a sense that any sudden motion will end him. Alexei weighs the odds, weighs the emptiness of the hangar, the dead certainty in her stance. He lowers the pry bar just a bit.

"I deliver to a dead drop," he says, teeth chattering from adrenaline. "It's always different. There's a code on my phone. They tell me where and when. I do not know who collects. I never see who. If you let me go, I'll—"

"You lie." Her eyes narrow to even blacker slits. "It will not help you," she says. "You always see. In the end, you always see."

Stepping backward, she returns outside. The door slams itself closed with a concussion of air. The hangar's lights—all of them—snuff out in a single, synchronized heartbeat.

Now it is only black, only the sound of his pulse in his ears, and her voice, everywhere and closer than before.

"We know you," she says. "We remember."

A single blinding light detonates over the center table. The metal surface is sanitized, every angle precise, every corner cold and clinical. He sees now what he couldn't before, the faint stains at the drain below. It is an altar to his own trade, his chosen profession.

He tries to run for the mechanics' caddies, but the air itself becomes glue, thickening, tugging at his feet. The ghosts are there—three of them, four, maybe more—faces not ruined but perfect, determined, the way they looked before he disposed of them. The girl from Cincinnati, the man from Moscow Mills, the desperate, lovely one from Oklahoma, a man and a woman from the motherland. They stand in a ring, hands out, palms empty, nothing but a void behind their eyes.

He tries to swing the pry bar, but his arm is slow, as if the world is running at quarter speed. They don't flinch, don't even track the motion. They just close in, step by step, silent as frost.

"It's our turn now," her ambient voice commands. "A chance to give back."

He resists or thinks he does. But the room is spinning, the walls flickering between pitch and light. The ghosts press him forward, not with force but with the inexorable certainty of something that cannot be bargained or reasoned with.

Alexei wants to scream. He wants to cut and run, or fight, or do anything except what is happening.

But in the end, it is simple. He is brought to the table. The light above washes out all detail, cold metal against his back. He knows, even as his vision is desperate for any out, that they will not kill him—not yet. They want something else. They want to know.

The Dead One looms over, its vaporous skull leers. The voices whisper, "Tell us."

No, this can't be. None of this—

Alexei closes his eyes and prays. Prays he will wake up.

Chapter Thirty-Three

Dark Questions

He keeps his eyes shut tight, the way a child does: the world can't find you if you refuse to look. But sensation, unlike sight, is impossible to will away. He is flat on the table. Alexei knows this by the pressure at his heels, the small of his back, the nape where the steel chills. The light above is so bright it is a physical force, boring through his eyelids, illuminating the thin red rivers in his capillaries.

And the hands. The hands are everywhere. Cold as wet meat, colder than any corpse he's ever handled, yet they clamp with the purposeful intent of living muscle. There are too many—one for every limb, and more. Some anchor his shoulders, others knot around his arms, two more flatten the thighs and pin the knees straight. Each grip is a little universe of force.

He tries to wrench free, to lurch upward, but the restraint is total. The ghosts—no, the dead—hold him as efficiently as any ER trauma team. He opens his mouth to scream, but something unseen shoves his jaw closed. The taste is of iron and chlorhexidine.

A voice—unbearably close, not quite human—worms into his left ear:

"Alexei."

He doesn't dare turn his head. He knows what awaits.

"We need you to answer," it says, and the vibration is in his skull, as if the voice resonates from the table itself.

He swallows.

Another voice, higher, female, fills the other side. "Tell us, Deliverer. Where do you deliver?"

He grits his teeth, refusing to dignify it with an answer.

A hand closes over his trachea—not choking, just applying enough pressure to make the intent clear. It's the hand of a young woman; he can feel the length of her fingers, the absence of a wedding band. The one from Oklahoma.

"Please," he says, first in English, then in Russian, "пожалуйста..."

The light above him pulses. The air is instantly so cold that he can see his breath.

The Dead One's voice, now doubled, crowds the world:

"You have a delivery to make. Where?"

He tries to shake his head, but the fingers on his skull hold him perfectly still. The dead are stronger than the living. The words tumble out, desperate, unfiltered.

"Never the same. It's arranged always with a code on the phone. There is a drop. They take, I go. That's all."

The one's hand on his throat relaxes, then tightens so fast he gags. In his left ear, a different voice hisses, "You're lying. You see them. Always see."

The thing leans over. Ghostly fingers pull his eyes open. The blinding light—it's impossible to discern its true shape, but there is a suggestion of a face, of a jaw, of negative space for the eyes.

"Then what is the code for tonight?" it demands.

Alexei's mind runs a rapid calculus: lie, or die. But the certainty is already there—these things know. They always know. He spits it out. "Delivery ten PM, same as always. They already told me where—" His voice cracks; he's forgotten how to breathe normally.

He senses movement: another hand, small and precise, places itself over his sternum. A cold so intense it is indistinguishable from a blade radiates into his chest.

The Dead One's face, now inches away, asks, "Where?"

He starts to cry. Not loudly; the tears leak without pride. "Gregg Cemetery," he sobs, "back entrance, south side. I'm to drop off there."

A chorus of whispers passes through the chamber. "The south entrance," "Gregg Cemetery," "He speaks truth," each with its own timbre, its own distinct pattern of resentment.

The Dead One is not yet done. "And the pickup?"

He shakes again. "Dumpster at the elementary school. Grab bag. Cash inside." His voice chokes.

The pressure in his chest builds until it feels like his heart is being iced, battered, then defibrillated by voltage.

The Dead One's voice softens, almost kind. "One more, Doctor. The code phrase."

He cannot stop the words. "This one's Saint-based. Valentines. Code Saint Valentine. Only speak in those terms. Please, please, you have it, you have everything."

He opens his eyes, desperate for mercy, and what he sees is a tribunal of faces: the faces of every donor, every patient he let fail, every victim, not raw and ragged as they were in death, but restored, vibrant, accusatory. They fill the hangar's heights, a dome of the once-were.

He looks up, mouth open, and tries to beg. "Mercy. Show mercy."

The dead release him, but only enough to let him see the Dead One's full height. It towers, arms outstretched, each finger now a glinting shard, curved and keen as a surgeon's blade.

"Mercy... I suppose," A chorus voice reverberates from its skull. "I suppose you would want us to... have a heart?"

Alexei screams.

Chapter Thirty-Four

Outside the Curve

L iam Hayes stands at the kitchen window, hand braced on the stainless steel sink, cold beer untouched. Outside, the river cuts a black vein through the patch of woods behind the subdivision; the world is night, open-throated and windless. He's not sure how long he's stared into the yard, watching the solar lights cycle through their faint colors.

He should be in bed. Liam should prep for his case review. He should not be waiting for a text from a woman who stopped answering him at the very moment she found what she was looking for. But that's the thing about hope: it kills slower than any bullet.

His phone faces down on the counter. He wants to flip it, see if the FBI has called, see if Evie has come to her senses or if some bureau bigwig has finally given the local badge a heads-up on what the hell is happening. Instead, he runs through the facts—again, as if repetition might fix the outcome:

Victims, all under thirty, all healthy, all harvested for high-value organs. Crossing multiple jurisdictions, no clear connection except the DNA markers Evie found. That's where the thread heated up and now sits expectantly.

He flips the phone.

No messages. He scrolls through the missed calls, then checks his email—nothing but procedural drivel and a single line from his boss: "Update when ready. Priority, Liam." He replies, "Still no word from the Bureau. Will follow up in the AM," and hits send.

He's about to close up and call it when the phone rings. Private number, but the tone is unmistakably in-state. He answers.

"Hayes."

The voice is his chief, half a county away but as present as if she were across the table. "You still on the Mills case?" she says.

He leans against the counter. "You have something?"

The chief exhales, and he knows it's not good. "Just got a call from Kansas City, the airport. Homicide got a new one inside one of the hangars. Local PD secured it, but they're requesting our involvement."

That knocks him off balance. "Airport? That's KCPD jurisdiction. Why us?"

"Because," she says, and he can picture her tapping the desk, "the body was apparently harvested. Clean, precise. Fits our pattern, Hayes."

He sets the beer down—hard. "Victim?"

"Male. White. Late thirties. No prints. KCPD says he's an illegal, possibly a recent entry. ICE had him on a deportation flight, headed to O'Hare, but he bolted. Last seen in cuffs, then next seen... not alive."

Liam breathes an audible sigh. "Don't suppose our FBI profiler is already on-hand?"

"Nope. I've got nothing on my end." The chief flips through papers. "What? Still nothing from her team?"

"Not so much." Hayes is silent for a beat. "Who's the responding detective?"

"Rourke. He'll play nice. But I need someone to represent by midnight. You're my guy."

Hayes looks at the clock on the stove: 10:51. The airport is two hours by road in ideal conditions, which is never, and the forecast says freezing drizzle at the line. "There's no way I'll make that in time."

"I've cleared it with the aviation office," she says, tone brisk. "Your bird is at the regional. You get there, and the State's dime will get you the rest of the way. You sober?"

Hayes looks at the untouched beer. "Yes, ma'am."

"Then get moving. Rourke is expecting you. Text me when you're airborne."

She hangs up before he can say thanks. Which is how he prefers it.

He's moving before he knows it, keys in hand, jacket zipped up against the cold. He snags the go-bag from the hall closet. The night air bites his face, sharp and unblinking. The old Ford is sluggish to start, but he's out of the driveway and down the highway in less than five minutes.

Their regional airport is a flat stretch of asphalt ringed by warehouses and self-storage. The security guard at the gate recognizes him, waves him through with the same old "Evenin', Detective" as if this is a Tuesday in July. His pilot is already seated, and the interior is warming.

He climbs in, buckles up, and takes a slow breath. The silence inside the cockpit is a living thing, broken only by the sound of his own pulse in his ears. At least until he dons the headphones. The air traffic chatter is so structured and rhythmic. At least there's order in that.

His pilot cycles the throttle, blades spinning overhead. With everything green, he radios the tower. "Highway Patrol Four-Five, requesting clearance for westbound to Kansas City International."

The tower operator comes back, polite but groggy. "Four-Five, you're cleared. Maintain six thousand, report passing Lake Lotawana."

"Copy. Four-Five up and away."

The pilot guides the chopper off the pad, noses west, and ascends. The world drops away beneath them. They bank toward the distant glitter of Kansas City, the engine's vibration settling into the base of Liam's spine.

Hayes has now a string of bodies, and a pattern waiting to make sense. Something awaits him at the airport. He hopes it's answers.

The helicopter surges forward, slicing through the wind, and Liam Hayes keeps his eyes fixed on the horizon, counting the minutes until that truth comes due.

Chapter Thirty-Five

Dead Drop

Gregg Cemetery, 22:04, late November.

Cole Danner kneels in the dry leaf litter behind the north wall, boots flat, breath low enough to pass for dead. The world here is in neutral, suspended far from the distant red taillights of Route 152. Not a good perimeter, but he's worked with less.

He checks his watch. Rhys had called the play to the second. "Window is 2200 to 2220, max," he'd said, "and I'll bet you a bottle it's closer to the front half." Cole had shrugged, not out of disagreement but because bets are sentimental, and he prefers a world scrubbed of them. You do the job, and if you win, you wake up again the next day.

The walkie is set to the lowest volume that will still breach skin when Rhys checks in. "Status?"

Cole huffs, then: "Eyes on. No strays at the north gate. Haven't seen much since the Honda five minutes ago. No movement since."

He scans across the scene. The picket fence is a tangle of dog rose and last year's grass. No animals, no wind. This necropolis buffers even the traffic sounds. The scent, if there is one, is only the vapor of Midwestern cold.

Shifting his position, slow and deliberately, Cole checks the gate wall: two meters tall, cinder block. At the base, a smudge that doesn't quite match the wall. Not new. Not old, either.

He thumbs the walkie again. "Any change on your six?"

Rhys's reply is immediate, almost bored: "Still in the yellow zone."

"Copy," Cole says. "On schedule."

He waits. The chill seeps through his knees, but his core remains motionless, ready. There is no edge of anticipation, no thrill of the chase, just a readiness—this is just a job. He's done worse things, in worse places, with less noble motivations.

The first sign is the pulse of white headlights up by the cross street. He doesn't need night optics for this; the Midwest is unkind to stealth, even at ten p.m. The vehicle—white, long, a faded Ford Econoline—slows, signals, then noses into the cemetery access road. He notes the lack of hesitation in the approach. A pro. Always a pro.

Cole's voice is quieter now, as if the air is thicker. "Van's on script. No U-turns, no hang backs."

The vehicle stops at the curb, engine idling.

The rear bay doors open. There is a slight sound of something heavy being pushed within, then the package is lowered to the ground. Van doors shut, and the vehicle wheels around and glides away, never once touching brake lights. In and out, the way it's supposed to go.

Cole counts to sixty, just in case. He scans the perimeter again, noting the absence of movement. Rhys has his side locked down.

He stands, rolls his neck, and approaches.

At two meters out, he pulls the disposable nitrile gloves from his pocket, slides them on. The air here is colder, and the ground beneath the leaves is frost-dry. He squats by what looks like a high-tech generator. There's a machine hum with a steady thump from within. He checks the digital readout of the heart-in-a-box machine. Cole knows how un-ironic that is named. The digital counter shows core temperature. He gives it a cautious tilt, listening for any slosh or unexpected heft. There is a sloshing, but it's contained, dense. Perfect.

He's been advised to inspect the contents briefly. Too much exposure increases risks, but not looking a 'gift horse' is a fool's move. Cole lifts the lid carefully. Inside, an opaque blue plastic sack, vacuumed and sealed, nested in a cage of electric heating packs. Connected to sterile hoses, the heart continues to beat with the pump aiding it. This is good. He checks the bag's seam for tampering. Nothing.

"Package is secure. Repeat, package is secured."

There's a brief pause, then: "Copy. Time to pay the man," Rhys says. "Meet at the exfil."

"Affirmative," says Cole. "East lot."

He reseals the package, and wipes the sidewalk for stray droplets. Nothing. Hefting it up by its industrial handles, Cole then retraces his steps, careful not to silhouette himself against the street lamps.

On the walk back, he lets his mind slip into the after-action. Not the job, but the method. Every trade like this is a test of protocol, of whether the other side is more ruthless, more disciplined, or more lucky. This one, like the last, was smooth. No hiccups, no attempt to double-cross, no wildcard. This Alexei—has a code. That's why they scouted him from that Texas beautician. It's a rare quality.

He covers his bases and stays mobile. It means he will live longer.

Rhys is waiting at the rendezvous, engine running, window cracked an inch to keep the glass from fogging.

"Was it him?" Rhys asks, even though Cole's already confirmed.

Cole swings the device onto the floor between his feet. "Signature matches. Package is good. You leave the payout?"

Rhys grins. "He delivers, and so do we. Waterproof bag dropped behind the dumpster. I almost felt bad; the bills looked so lonely."

"Nobody's coming to collect until we're gone," Cole says.

"You're such an optimist," Rhys answers, and eases the car into gear.

They take the roundabout to the airport, keeping the speed just under the limit. On the surface, it's just two guys in a rental, driving nowhere special. However, there'd be no explaining away their cargo if it got searched. Cole tends not to worry too much about it, but he's prepared to end the situation before it starts... if it comes to that.

As they pass the last stoplight before the access road, Rhys looks over. "You ever think about our end user? Who's worth this much trouble for a viable heart?"

Cole doesn't consider. He already knows. "Not part of the job."

Rhys laughs, but it's dry. "That's why they keep us."

The regional airfield is a flat grid of tarmac and security lights. The FBO manager meets them at the curb, clipboard and no need for IDs. Rhys does the talking while Cole handles the cargo, walking it onto the tarmac, protecting like a 70 lb. newborn. The jet is waiting, copilot at the bottom of the stairs.

Cole acknowledges the pilot as he climbs the steps. "Wheels up. We're out." At the stair top, he glances back before ducking inside. They are the sole passengers. As it should be.

Rhys clearly cuts his chat short, seeing the pilot getting ready to raise the stairs. He scrambles past him and into the cabin. His frown precedes him into the back of the Pilatus jet. Cole is already seated and buckled, package secured in its own seat.

"We in a hurry?" Rhys asks.

Cole nods.

Rhys flumps into the seat across. He runs his hands through his thinning hair and lolls back up with a smirk. "God damn. The Deliverer never misses."

Cole leans to peer out the window. "No. He never does."

The engine revs up, and the Pilatus taxis away. Just a single runway here. No tower. No record. As it should be.

Cole Danner knows his place in the chain, and as long as the job demands men like him, he'll keep the balance. He'll keep the world turning, one perfect delivery at a time.

Man, the Deliverer always delivers.

Chapter Thirty-Six

Just Not Right

Liam's view from the chopper is a kaleidoscope of airport lighting on one side of the hangar and emergency vehicle lightbars on the other. Hayes squints out the passenger window, watching the swirl of blue-red pulses, a tight barricade of cruisers and fire units boxing the entire building off from the outside. Every now and then, the flash from a news van strobes the building's exterior.

They land on the hangar apron, away from the media lines. His pilot gives a wordless salute; Hayes takes his go-bag and steps out into a wind that cuts through his wool coat and denim. A patrolman waits by the perimeter tape, gloved hands jammed under his armpits. He doesn't speak, just tips his chin toward the side entrance.

Inside the tape, a city detective paces the gravel. The man is thin, with a face that suggests nicotine more than sleep. He clocks Hayes immediately, reads the plain suit, the boots, the badge pinched to the belt. "State Highway?" he says, like he's picking out a vendor from a police buffet.

"Detective Hayes," he replies.

They shake hands. "Detective Tom Rourke." He leads him in, down a corridor of cinderblock and insulation board. "Scene's about as pure as it gets. They cordoned off the hangar as soon as airport security found the body. Only ones in are the forensics."

"How long since?" Hayes asks.

"Hour-forty, or so. No one's touched the vic. No need to check for a pulse."

They step into the hangar proper. It's been repurposed for airport maintenance but sits empty—a dozen toolboxes line the wall, a few hydraulic lifts squat in the shadows. All the high-bay LED fixtures bathe every square inch of the concrete surface.

The body lies on its back, arms hanging out at the sides, ribcage splayed open like dead spider legs. His clothing is intact except for the split-open shirt. The chest is a yawning pit. Blood—more than Hayes has seen in years—spreads from the cavity in a perfect, glossy disk, maybe four feet in diameter. The face is turned slightly left, the eyes open and so pale they almost seem to fluoresce in the harsh light.

A forensics team orbits at the perimeter: a pathologist in blue nitrile, a younger woman snapping photos from every angle, a blood spatter tech with an iPad, and a third, more senior CSI handling the perimeter with tape and evidence flags. No one stands closer than six feet from the table, except the pathologist, who hunches over the body, making notes.

Hayes steps up, keeping just outside the evidence cones. "You the medical?"

The pathologist glances up, her nose and mouth pressed behind an N95. "For the time being. Until the coroner shows." Her eyes are brown, keen, and unimpressed. "You're the outside assist?"

Hayes nods. "What am I looking at here?"

She motions for him to step around. "Victim is Alexei Volkov, Bosnian illegal, male, thirty-two. Hands are clean. Dress is jeans, a polo shirt, and athletic jacket." She motions with a capped Sharpie. "He was, in all probability, conscious at the time of incision. If you could stand where I am, you'd see—" She points to the edges of the chest cavity, where the skin has curled back. "This wasn't done with a surgical bone saw. There are no striations. Very clean-cut, though—almost like lasered, but without any scorching."

The blood spatter tech chimes in, "A few cast-offs, notably on the ventral side. And the edges here—" He points at the pooling around the victim's right shoulder—"that's all gravity. No struggle, no movement after the big cut."

Hayes makes a mental note, then turns to the pathologist. "The heart?"

"Oh, yeah. Gone," she says. "Removed completely. Major vessels were left open, gaping. Amateur, but precise cuts. Whoever did this had at least basic anatomy."

Liam lifts himself onto his toes, craning for any additional view. The ribs are split with cruel symmetry. He lets his eyes follow the arc of blood out, then around the table. Except for a few sprays, it is perfectly circular, without the usual splash or spatters.

He looks back at the rest of the forensics team, all of whom are standing outside the perimeter. The air is frosty, but he's seen techs crowd worse scenes in unventilated trailer homes.

He turns to Detective Rourke. "Why's everyone standing off?"

"You see any footprints in that blood?"

Hayes looks. There are none. Not even a heel drag, not a scuff, nothing but the pathologist's two crisp ovals, tracked straight in, none stepping back.

"We dusted the perimeter," the CSI says, "and checked the floor with luminol before the team entered. Nothing but his shoes and ours." She steps over, toggling through a handheld scanner. "It's not just the blood. There's no trace of fiber, hair, or even particulates from the HVAC. It's like the body just ran in here and laid itself down."

Hayes rubs the back of his neck. "No wheel marks, no gurney?"

"Nothing," she says. "Door logs show entry from airport security at 8:03. Prior to that, there was a hit at the hanger door and back door at 7:26. Last janitorial access was 6:17."

He walks a slow circle around the table, careful to avoid the pooling blood. "Who found him?"

"Paid security, guy named Miller," Rourke says. "Had a sensor on the main door, but the back door was opened by hitting the bar from the inside. When the airport EMT arrived, they saw the body and knew well enough to leave it. No one else entered until KCPD. Then we suited up and brought in the doc."

Hayes pinches the bridge of his nose. "Time of death?"

"Pretty fresh, right within the window before discovery," the pathologist says. "Temperature's ambient with the room, but blood viscosity suggests less than an hour post-mortem. Means he was killed here and staged immediately—somehow without making a big mess."

"Any evidence of forced entry?" Hayes asks, standing.

"None," the CSI says. "Every lock, every latch intact. The exterior security cams show a power loss of about 30 minutes before coming back online. Not a hard guess to figure out what was going on during."

Hayes considers this. He thinks of the cold out there, the silence of the hangar, the wild physics of a body placed with no prints, no mess. He glances at the forensics team again. "Anyone see anything... off?"

Rourke snorts. "You mean besides a body with no heart and a clean circle of blood?"

"I mean, any unusual signatures. Smells, sights, anything you'd usually ignore."

The pathologist looks at him for a second. "There's a smell," she says. "Like... freezer burn. Very faint, but I clocked it as soon as I got close."

"Could be a chemical agent?"

She shrugs. "If it is, it's not one I know."

Hayes files that away. He kneels, scanning the floor for anything missed, then stands again, stretching out the ache in his knees. "You said there was a power outage?"

The CSI flips through her phone. "Yeah, recorded by the main server. We checked—a partial brownout. Every other suite on the grid was unaffected."

Hayes nods, slow. "You got a technician to walk me through the cam logs?"

"I can bring up the feed," the CSI says.

They step to the side of the room, away from the working team. The CSI thumbs her phone and brings up a split-screen of the entry. She hands it over, and Hayes watches as, at exactly 07:12:11, both cameras go dark. The timestamp freezes, then, after the jump, resumes at 07:42:48. Then, at 08:03, airport security arrives, their flashlights sweeping the grounds.

Hayes rewinds, watching the jump again. "Does it buffer off-site?"

"Yes," she says, "but it's the same gap in the cloud backup."

He hands back the phone. "So, our guy got in and out during that window."

The CSI smiles, dry. "The timing is perfectly plausible."

Hayes shrugs and strides back toward the scene. "But that blood pool—" He gestures. "That's not rage. That's frigging magic."

Rourke shoves his hands in his pockets. "So, is your serial killer a professional?"

Hayes shakes his head. "Professionals don't work in the open, and they don't advertise. This is something else."

He returns to the pathologist. "You know what's going to happen, right? As soon as this hits the database, every suit in the Tri-State is going to want a piece."

She nods. "It's not the first time."

He scans the body once more, forcing himself to look at the details. The jaw is unshaven, lips pale and bloodless. The victim's eyes frozen in terror. What would it take to bring a man down, bleed him dry, and leave no trace of movement?

That's when Evie wanders back into his thoughts. Of her fractured calm, her recursive logic. He wonders, if she were here, would she see anything different?

Rourke, perhaps sensing the spiral, cuts in. "We're still pulling the footage from the terminal. Also, we've got his ICE chaperone we're keeping at EMT. Figured I'd wait, so we don't have to sit with them twice."

Hayes closes his notepad. "If you wouldn't mind sparing a copy of everything? I'd also like to send a tech from State to sit in tomorrow."

Rourke shrugs. "Knock yourself out. Frankly, I'd be thrilled to let this be someone else's headache."

Hayes half smiles. "Doubt that'll be me once the Feds swoop in."

"Shall we get going?" Rourke gestures toward the side exit.

Hayes nods. "Lead the way."

As they exit, Hayes casts one last look over the shoulder. The forensics team still stands at a distance, as if the body is going to get up and walk away. He gets the feeling that if it did, none of them would be surprised.

He follows Rourke out into the wind, already writing the next report in his head, already trying to predict what the FBI will want to know. He's not going to text Evie—not yet—but the thought sits with him, sharp as the cold.

The only thing worse than a puzzle with no pieces is the certainty that every new piece will make the picture worse.

He braces for it anyway.

Chapter Thirty-Seven

The Deliverer

The school sits behind a line of hackberry trees, their trunks nearly indistinguishable in the November dark. Across the road, hunkered low behind a cluster of utility boxes, Evie becomes a fixed point, her presence dissolved into the cold. She wears three layers under her jacket, but the wind needles through anyway.

She checks her watch. 9:11. Plenty of time. The drop isn't until 10:00, and more than likely this buyer's expectations are quite rigid. Her time with the Bureau taught being too early is a lesser sin than being late. Especially in someone else's play.

The binoculars are not high-end, but they're enough. She uses them to scan the rows of teacher parking, the playground equipment, the double-stacked dumpsters at the far edge. There's no movement at first. Just the gentle breeze on the yellowing grass, and the slight swaying of the parking lights. The rope of the flagpole was left slack. Its clasp makes a hollow, tubular resonance from each tap.

She takes shallow breaths, each one misting away in the wind. Her mind wants to spiral into the metaphysical: the sense of being watched, the echo of the Harbinger's chill somewhere within. But she forces herself into procedure, the weight and comfort of it. She mentally rehearses the expected: the runner will park, scan the surroundings, wait for confirmation of delivery, drop off and clear out. If they sense anything or anyone out of the ordinary, they'll burn it all down.

At 9:23, a dark sedan rolls slow down the street, then pulls a full U-turn before easing into the school lot. The car is unremarkable, but Evie clocks it instantly as a rental—the interior still has the tags on the passenger seatbelt, and the rear window shows a sticker for Enterprise. She tracks the plate, writes it into her notebook: MO, 5XE 3K2.

The driver waits a full five minutes before killing the lights and opening the door. She makes a mental note: patient, methodical. Whoever is running this is good.

He's a white male, early to late 30s, athletic but fraying at the edges. He gets out with a duffel bag and drops it on the hood. Lighting a cigarette, he walks the perimeter of the lot, eyes never resting too long in one direction.

After the circuit, he returns to the car and leans against the fender with his smoke. He does a walkie check-in—she sees the glint of the antenna as he keys the mic. The conversation is brief, just a head-tilt and a nod. He's waiting for confirmation or an all-clear.

That's all she needs for now. Evie stows the binoculars, draws in a long, cold breath, and melts backward into the line of trees. Each step is calculated, her footfalls matched to the shuddering branches overhead.

She doesn't look back.

It's six minutes to the rental van, parked two blocks down a residential street. Then she's on stage two.

Her drive to the cemetery is uneventful, but circuitous—a three-mile vein of residential, then a left at a shuttered gas station and through an underpass painted with spray-can saints. A white rail fence outlines Gregg Cemetery. It's as unremarkable as every other plot in Missouri: half a dozen family plots with a lone memorial bench, and a single access turnoff.

She backs into an arc of the drive, engine running, headlights illuminating the foremost headstones. It's just enough for the vehicle's tail end to hang over the grass. The cargo van's lack of insulation retains no warmth away from the heater. She pivots out of her seat and into the rear compartment. Alexei's high-end "heart-in-a-box" machine's LEDs cast a faint blue from its temperature readout. She squats before it, letting her pulse decelerate, eyes adjusting to the faint glow of the medical unit.

Evie allows herself a brief pause to prep.

The damned thing weighs seventy pounds. It's not like her 110-pound ballerina frame is going to step out into the open and lug it to the ground. Besides it being just too heavy, it would also be way too revealing of who she is not!

Thankfully, Home Depot had her answer: Evie lashed two sets of webbing to E-track rails and fitted a paracord harness around the cooler's handles. She spent a solid half an hour practicing the system so that she could lower the machine without toppling or dragging.

It isn't perfect, but it'll suffice.

She grips the webbing in her gloved hands, pulls the quick-release to slide the device toward the rear. The heart-in-a-box is a little larger than an airline carry-on, but has a density like a baby mule. She braces her knees, leans into the tension, and shoves it the final six inches to the edge of the van floor.

A flick of the wrist, and the rear doors yawn open. She doesn't bother to check the perimeter—from inside the darkened cab, no one could see her anyway.

Evie unlocks the pulley, letting the cooler descend until it's level with the bumper. She holds it there, letting gravity do the work, then releases the second set of webbing. The cooler settles to the ground with a muted thunk, the reinforced polymer bottom absorbing the impact.

She leans out, never letting her shoes cross the threshold. With a practiced hook of her gloved hand, she retracts the cords, stows them, and closes the doors with a silent, two-handed pull.

Returning to the driver's seat, Evie slouches low, and checks the side mirror. Nothing and no one. Not once does she give this contractor a silhouette to work with.

All right. Onto stage two.

Evie rolls the van back onto the access road. She takes the right, a slow glide through a sleepy rural setting. Much like where she grew up. She wonders for a moment how many people have ever known what passes through their neighborhoods at night. The thought is both comforting and sad.

The school's parking lot is empty.

She backs up alongside the rusted blue dumpster. Embracing the warmth of the running engine's heater. A quick sensory sweep: the parking lot is a grid of empty rectangles, no movement near the building, the playground underlit and quiet. Nothing but the slow applause of bare hackberry branches.

Evie rolls out, boots hitting blacktop with a slick tap. The parking lot's lighting washes over the dumpster and the worn strip of asphalt behind it. She moves fast, uncoiling herself along the rear wall.

Their comms said it would be here, and so it is—a black duffel, the kind that would pass for a gym bag if not for the plastic tamper-evident lash through the zipper. Honestly, if their boss wanted to ensure his contractors wouldn't skim, he shouldn't have provided a zipper duffle. There are easy ways around that.

Evie crouches, retrieves the bag. It's heavier than expected. With a pocket knife, she snaps the loop and inspects it. Bricks of bundled twenties and hundreds, crisp as if first time in circulation, fill the interior. She makes a fast assessment; most are 20s, about six or seven are 100s. Evie hauls the duffle back to the van, and climbs in.

She's never done this before—handled contraband. It's certainly not like tracking the flow of money from a spreadsheet. Yet, the only thing that matters now is the endgame.

This will lead to that.

Back at the van, she sits in the dark for a moment, feeling the charge of the night finally ebb. Then she pulls her phone, scrolls to the tracker app, and checks the ping.

There it is: a single blue dot, moving steadily west on State Route 45, just outside of Waldron. The GPS is perfect—she'd triple-wrapped the tracker, and slipped it inside the cooler's components, set to update every five seconds. She stares at the dot for a full minute, mesmerized by its persistence.

Evie shifts the van into gear and heads west, following the blue dot into the dark.

She doesn't know whether the Harbinger rides with her, or if it's even necessary anymore.

She's got her vector, and the intent to follow.

All that's left... is Mercer.

Chapter Thirty-Eight

Comes Full Circle

Kansas City International's security office is nothing like on television. No sleek glass, no floating map of the United States. Just wood paneling, carpet older than the city's newest landfill, and the drab, choked hum of fluorescents. Rourke and Hayes sit elbow to elbow in a conference space half-commandeered by city suits, county sheriffs, and a scattering of commercial security with pastel shirts.

On the far wall, a battered flatscreen plays back security camera footage. Six angles, tiled. The digital clock in the corner advances in stutters, each freeze-frame its own grim slide in a lecture no one wants to attend.

Hayes keeps his focus on the images: the jetway, empty except for two figures. Parsons teams up with another ICE officer to lead Volkov through the concourse. Alexei walks with stoic patience, shoulders canted back, face unreadable even at this resolution. As common, she has covered Volkov's cuffs with a windbreaker not to draw attention. The moment they reach a glass corridor, there's a visible stutter—a hitch in his stride. Parsons responds to him, looks back, then continues.

The clock ticks forward.

"Here," says Rourke, pointing as Parsons and Volkov move again, now toward their departure gate.

The footage is clinical, even boring, until it isn't.

At 19:18:11, Parsons touches her face, then her nose. Her hand comes away with a bright red smear, clearly visible even through the pixel haze. She wobbles, knees buckling. Volkov, in that split-second, turns toward her. The motion is so quick it looks like a tape glitch.

At 19:18:14, Parsons is on the carpet. Volkov stands there for a beat, frozen. There's a shimmer in the video feed as Volkov shifts. At first it looks like nervous fidgeting, but then the handcuffs fall from under the windbreaker—

"Pause that," says one of the county guys. He leans in. "Did he pick the lock?"

The contract suit beside him shakes his head. "Those are mil-spec cuffs."

"Must've been a cheap pair," snorts another.

Rourke rewinds the feed, frame by frame. He and Hayes lean in.

There's nothing to make out with the windbreaker covering. The cuffs just... appear. No visible movement. No noticeable sleight of hand.

A suit from the back—the ICE regional manager grunts, "Maybe Parsons didn't double-lock it."

"That's not it," says Rourke, voice flat.

"Guy was spooked," another ICE manager chimes in. "He was voluntarily being deported. Was not even thinking about escape, not until the moment Parsons goes down. Something happened there."

They roll the video. Volkov sprints down the hall, and the camera jumps to the service corridor. He's through it in seconds. His feet slip on the vinyl, but he never goes down. He ducks a janitor cart, nearly barrels over a family of four. The software blurs the faces, but the effect is cartoonish—everyone else is running on tape delay; Volkov is running at three times normal speed.

"Must've been high," someone offers.

Hayes shakes his head. "He was in lock-up for twenty-four. The only thing he could be high on is adrenaline."

Another camera picks up the trail: Volkov out a staff exit, then cutting across the baggage lane, vaulting a waist-high wall with the panache of a military vet. In the next frame, he's through a security gate and out onto the tarmac.

"That's the last we had of him," the security office manager says. "Ground units started a sweep, but there's too much real estate to cover fast." He glances at Hayes. "Guy ran like he was being hunted."

Leaning forward, Hayes asks Rourke to roll the scene back. He's looking for the exact moment everything goes off-script. When Volkov enters the open, his head never stops scanning—left, right, up, then back. He's running from something, but not airport staff. When his cuffs fall, he's looking up—not vacantly, but seemingly at something as his eyes widen.

Hayes shifts back in the seat. The others keep spit-balling: theories about drugs, about possible inside help, even the notion that Volkov had accomplices waiting outside the perimeter. It's all noise. No, there's something else he's looking for. Was it a camera? A sniper? Hayes is searching for a shadow in the footage, a ghost in the pixels.

The suits start getting bored. One by one, they take calls in the hall, check phones, argue about jurisdiction. The only ones who stay glued to the screen are Hayes, Rourke, and the forensics girl from earlier.

"Rewind again, twenty seconds before Parsons drops," says Hayes. Rourke does it. They watch in silence.

There, far down the corridor, in the glare from a side window, stands a figure in the crowd. A woman, gray jacket, with a slight frame, hair coiled in familiar twists. Her face is half turned, but it's enough. Liam's stomach drops—vertigo teeters at him. How is she here?

He's the only one who notices. The only one who could.

Liam doesn't speak.

Instead, he files it away. A question, a lead, maybe a warning. But this room is not the place for it.

The rest of the night is interviews, paperwork, and jurisdictional arm-wrestling. Rourke is professional, but he's tired, and Hayes can feel the itch to wrap up the mess and pass it along the bureaucratic food chain.

Before sunrise, the first news reports will hit the wires: ICE detainee escape, but body recovered. Police investigating. The victim is not named. Hayes wonders if that'll hold, or if someone will leak the autopsy report.

He stays until the local ME wraps, then steps outside. Liam checks his phone. No new calls, but the last message from Evie burns on the screen: 'All good. Will update once things pan out.'

The Detective in him has no more reason to wait.

> LIAM: Saw something today. Tell me you're safe.

No reply. Not at first.

He spends the next hour with airport security, asking for digital copies of every frame from the relevant cameras. They're slow about it, but they will comply. It's not until his drive back to the hotel that his phone buzzes.

> EVIE: Not safe, but not lost. Following something bigger. Promise I'll explain.

He reads it a dozen times, parsing for code, for fear, for any secret she's smuggled in. But it's just her. Stubborn, fixated, asking him to believe.

He wants to.

> LIAM: If you need help, say the word. Any time. I'll come.

This time, the silence feels longer. He pulls into the hotel lot, engine ticking.

Her reply comes:

> EVIE: Thank you. Kinda hope it comes to that.

He doesn't press it.

The night is raw, and his room is dingier than most jails, but he's slept in worse. Liam throws his jacket on the bed, unpacks the case file, and spends another hour sketching out the pattern. Not for the Bureau, not for the case, but for himself: he needs to see the outline of what she's chasing.

He's half through his notes when the phone rings. This time, it's not a private number, but a local prefix—his boss.

He answers. "Hayes."

It's not his boss. State Captain Eli Forrester's old man's voice is a gravel pit, and there's no preamble. "Detective. You know this airport case is going to blow up in our faces, right?"

Hayes sits, pen poised. "I expect as much. KCPD is on the job. I'm going to review the footage again and confer with them after I get some rest."

"Well, I need more than the local PD. You're going to lead the search. KCPD can handle their end, but I need someone with a brain and a backbone. As far as I'm concerned, this is your op now. We'll authorize whatever you need."

"Understood," says Hayes. It should feel like a win. It doesn't.

Forrester lowers his voice, as if the line is wiretapped. "I'm expecting Bureau red tape. I expect you'll do your political best. But, Hayes, I need someone's hide on this. You're my man."

"Got it," Hayes says. "I am your man."

A pause, then: "Glad to hear. Keep me in the loop."

The line goes dead.

He sits for a while, the legal pad growing heavier in his hands.

At 7:17, he calls to check on the requested footage. They're now to route it to his personal account, and give them a plausible story about prepping for a multi-jurisdictional task force. No one questions it.

At 7:22, he checks the window. The parking lot is empty.

He books his room for another night, then settles in and draws the blackout curtains closed.

The phone buzzes once, twice.

He answers on the second.

A man's voice, older, smooth, yet with a core of warning.

"Detective Hayes? This is Special Agent Thomas Haden."

Hayes doesn't speak. His words hang, like a breath about to be exhaled.

"Detective?" repeats the voice, with the sort of patience only federal training can buy.

Hayes releases the breath. "Yes. Go ahead."

Spectral Hunter: Book 3

Once hailed as a prodigious FBI profiler, Evie Cross embodies a woman tormented by an enigma and inhabited by an ancient entity beyond retribution. Now, she must journey deep into the mountains to confront the ruthless powerbroker who has eluded her at every turn. Alexander Mercer is no stranger to death—but this time, could it be his own life at stake?

The boundaries between prey and predator blur, and the toll of retribution threatens to consume her very essence. Empowered by the supernatural and hunted by her own team, Evie must determine how deep she will venture to unveil her daughter's fate—and whether the fragments of her being are salvageable.

In a gripping tale of darkness and salvation, Evie must face her own demons to vanquish the most formidable monster of all—the one she risks becoming. The truth is closer than ever. And so is the point of no return.

"An electrifying supernatural saga delving into the ethereal balance between morality and payback. THIS VANTA MIRROR will enthrall you from its captivating inception to its haunting resolution."

Amazon: Jan. 2, 2026

Submit a Review

I f **Harvest Protocol** resonated with you, a short review on Amazon would mean the world to me. It helps other readers discover the story and supports my work. Share what you loved most (a favorite scene, character, or moment that stayed with you) and whether you'd recommend it; even a sentence or two makes a huge difference.

Thank you for taking a moment to leave your thoughts—your voice helps this book find its next reader.

Also from ALVS

The Books of Ruein
Death has its own kind of grace.

When the gods stopped listening, Ruein learned to whisper to the dead.

Once a mother, wife, and reluctant necromancer, she has clawed her way through curses, godless realms, and divine betrayals to protect the one thing that still matters—her family. But every spell cast in love carries a shadow, and Ruein's has begun to stir.

From the smoke of Vandraport's streets to the frozen citadels of Haraden, Ruein is hunted by powers both mortal and celestial. To save her son, she'll forge impossible alliances: with dragons, killers, and even the Lightbringer sworn to destroy her. Yet the deeper she delves into the underworld of magic, the more she risks becoming what she most fears.

Because the dead are never done with you.

Wickedly funny, brutal, and unflinchingly human, The Books of Ruein is a dark fantasy saga of necromancy, faith, and the cost of love in a world that eats its own gods.

For readers of The Witcher, The First Law, and The Sandman, who prefer their fantasy rich with blood, ash, and gallows humor.

Now Available on Amazon

UFO Science
Unraveling the Phenomena

Step beyond speculation and into discovery. The UFO Science Series takes you on an unprecedented exploration of the evidence, physics, and mysteries shaping humanity's understanding of Unidentified Anomalous Phenomena and the enigmatic patterns that appear in our fields.

In Book One, uncover the revolutionary science that may drive advanced UAP craft. From declassified Pentagon encounters to breakthrough theories by pioneers like T. Townsend Brown and Jack Sarfatti, you'll gain a clear and comprehensive view of the physics that could be redefining reality itself.

In Book Two, delve into the geometric and biological mysteries of crop circles—where intricate designs meet scientific data. Explore soil anomalies, eyewitness accounts, and the unexplained precision behind these vast formations that continue to defy conventional reasoning.

Blending research, case studies, and cutting-edge hypotheses, this series challenges readers to look closer, think deeper, and question what they thought they knew about the world around them.

The frontier of discovery is here.

Are you ready to see what's been hiding in plain sight?

Now Available on Amazon